A percentage of the profits from *The Brother's Creed* series will be donated to Colors of Heroes®.

Freedom is never free!

Colors of Heroes is a 501c3 nonprofit foundation dedicated to rebuilding confidence for combat wounded veterans and gold star families through new relationships and outdoor adventures.

Learn more at: *www.colorsofheroes.org*

OUTBREAK

THE BROTHER'S CREED
BOOK 1

JOSHUA C. CHADD

Published in the United States by Blade of Truth
Publishing Company

Cover art by Biram Ba

Contact the author via email at:
joshuacchadd@outlook.com

ISBN-13: 978-1545062333

ISBN-10: 1545062331

Caleb,
I'll always have your back and I know you will
mine. Brothers till we die!

~~~

For all her support over the years, no matter what
frivolous things I was pursuing. She has always
been there to guide me, help me to know what is
right, and put me back on the road I was meant to
wander.
For always encouraging and nurturing my
imagination, whether with movies, books, or my
own writing. She has always helped me open my
mind and not be ashamed of my dorky and nerdy
side. I would not be, could not be, the man or the
writer I am today without her.

This one's for you mom

1
FIRST ENCOUNTER

A shot echoed throughout the gas station, followed shortly by another. A young man cautiously approached his targets, making sure they were indeed dead; both bodies had bullet holes in their heads. He moved through the rest of the station gathering supplies, always keeping his handgun close. When he was done, he went back outside and climbed into the passenger seat of a white truck parked next to the pumps.

"You get anything good?" his brother asked him.

"No, just the usual—a few canned goods and what have you. Nothing worth shouting over," he said, throwing the grocery bags into the backseat. "Let's roll out."

As they sped down the highway, he couldn't help but smile. They were off to a great start. In the backseat were three cases of water and a pile of non-perishable food, along with two rifles and two shotguns, not to mention the beautiful blonde woman who returned his smile when he glanced back.

He looked down at the AR-15 that rested next to his seat. It was a gorgeous firearm that had been through a lot lately. But never would he have imagined it being used to kill zombies, and yet it had done a lot more than that in the last day…

The day had started off like any other summer day for James and Connor Andderson. They'd awakened early, doing a quick workout before breakfast, and then packed their things. They were going out to the ranch for the weekend to do some prairie dog and coyote hunting. Loading all their gear and guns into James's truck, they then got on their computers for a quick update.

A couple days earlier there had been several brutal murders in Hill City, Texas. Then, yesterday, Hill City had gone dark. Shortly after, the state troopers had been sent in and nothing had been heard from them since. When the same thing started happening in other towns in eastern Texas last night, the National Guard had been sent in. Now there were rumors and videos circulating the internet.

The dead were coming back to life.

Of course, all the doomsayers were claiming zombies and the end of the world, but the more rational public wasn't buying it. Most of the media claimed some crap about state-wide power outages. However, today there was new information that other states were experiencing similar scenarios.

"Have you read this yet?" James asked his brother, pointing to the article on his screen. James was the older brother at twenty-one with short brown hair, hazel eyes, and an athletic build.

Connor came over and started reading. He had his brown hair in a buzz cut and was the younger brother by two years but was both taller and more muscular. The resemblance between the two, however, was striking, and they had often been asked if they were twins when they were younger.

"This is getting serious," Connor said as he headed over to the phone. "I'm giving Mom and Dad a quick call to let them know we'll be gone for the weekend."

James read the rest of the article, which claimed that none of the incidents were in any way related and that it was just coincidence. He didn't believe that for a second. The article was by CCN, and they never told the truth. *It's probably terrorists,* he thought. *Well, they won't catch us with our pants down.*

Connor hung up the phone. "They said not to worry about them, that this will blow over soon, and to have fun hunting."

"Good. No use burnin' more daylight then. Let's hit the road and go shoot something!" James shut his laptop and slipped it back in the case. Putting their boots on, they grabbed the last box of ammo before heading out the door.

"We get everything?" James asked as he climbed into the driver's seat.

"Of course we did. You already triple checked!"

"Hey, you can never be too sure, bro."

They pulled out, starting down their dirt driveway, and headed to town. Twenty minutes later they stopped for fuel in Cowtown, a small settlement in the plains of eastern Montana, where they filled up and got back on the road.

They arrived at their hunting camp in the heart of the ranch at noon and unloaded the truck, putting their clothes in the bunk cabin, food in the cook shack, and guns in a green Ford Expedition aptly named *the Death Wagon*. A little while later they were making dust fly down the bumpy dirt road to the first prairie-dog town. Pulling up to a small rise above the dog town, James parked *the Death Wagon*. Getting out, they grabbed their AR-15s from beside them. Their ARs were things of beauty, with collapsible buttstocks, foregrips, bipods, and attachments on the rails for flashlights. Connor's was a Bushmaster, with a sixteen-inch barrel and a 4x32 Trijicon ACOG optic, while James's was an S&W with a sixteen-inch barrel and 1-4x24 Vortex illuminated scope.

They each shoved a magazine into their rifles and jacked a round into the chamber. Lying prone, they looked down at the prairie-dog town spread before them.

"I have two spotted," James said, "about two hundred yards out. Go to the right of the lone tree about ten yards, then down a little."

"Got 'em," Connor said before James could finish talking. "You take the one on the left and I'll get the one on the right. You lead."

James had his crosshairs resting on the vermin the whole time Connor had been talking. When Connor finished, James slowly exhaled and squeezed the trigger. The prairie dog did a backflip as the fifty-five-grain bullet collided with its body. Before the dog could land, Connor let a round fly, blowing the head off the other one.

"Good shot!" James said, congratulating his brother. "Okay, I got another set a little farther out, three hundred yards this time. The big black hole, straight out."

Connor's confirmation came a second later. "Target acquired. I'll take point this time, same side as always."

Aiming through their scopes at their prospective prairie dogs, they rested their reticles on the vermin. The shots were less than a second apart, and both dogs were dead after the dust settled. They continued for the next few hours, picking out prairie dogs and blasting them. They didn't always hit their mark, but the next time they made sure to correct their aim and not "jerk" the trigger.

At the end of the day, back at camp, they cooked up a hearty dinner of venison. They had shot close to two hundred rounds each and killed almost as many prairie dogs. It had been a good day of hunting, and they ate while watching *Shooter* on the small TV at camp before going to bed.

The next morning, they went out early to coyote hunt, killing three. During the middle of the day they were out prairie dog hunting again, as the rodents liked it when it was hot. All in all, the brothers spent a beautiful weekend at the ranch.

On Monday, they closed camp and loaded everything back into James's truck. They bumped along the rugged dirt road and finally made their way onto the paved road that led into town, but when they pulled into town around eight a.m. they hadn't passed a single vehicle.

"This is weird," James mumbled as he drove toward Main Street, heading for the grocery store.

Turning the corner, they gasped. The street was littered with abandoned cars. Some had crashed into buildings and others looked like they had been left in a hurry. But that wasn't the worst of it; there were bodies—*dead bodies*—lying all over the street and slouched in the vehicles.

"What the…" James said as he took in the scene.

"What happened here?" Connor asked.

The first body they reached was lying face down in the middle of the street. They got out of the truck, grabbing their holstered handguns and slipping them onto their belts. Slowly, they approached the body.

"Hey? Are you okay?" James asked.

He was bending down to examine the body when the smell hit him. It was the stench of meat rotting in the hot sun. He'd smelled it before, but only with animals, never humans.

Connor's training began to kick in. As a Marine he'd been trained to survive, and even though his military career had been cut short and he'd never seen combat, his instincts were still strong. He was treating this like a warzone, except something wasn't right. If this was an attack by another country, where were all the soldiers? Or did this have something to do with all the blackouts? He couldn't put his finger on it, but something was terribly wrong with this situation.

James rolled the body over while Connor stayed two steps behind, hand resting on the gun at his hip.

"Holy…" James said, covering his mouth with his hand. The corpse was bloated, with a gaping wound at his neck and a hole in his head. "He's been here at least a day. And bro, he's been shot in the head."

"We need to get back to the truck and get out of here," Connor said with an edge to his voice. Something was *definitely* not right.

"I agree," James said, standing to follow his brother back towards the truck.

Something groaned behind them.

Connor began to turn around while drawing his gun, and James followed suit. There was nothing there—only the bodies scattered on the street.

"What was that?" James asked.

"I don't know but—there!" Connor said, pointing to movement ten yards away. It was one of the bodies, and judging by the long black hair and delicate physique, it looked to be a woman.

"Someone's alive!" James cried out, running toward the woman and holstering his gun.

Connor followed.

The woman rolled over and began to rise on unsteady legs.

"Don't move! We're coming to you!" James shouted as he closed in. He was only three steps away when he came to a sudden halt, his eyes growing wide.

The woman was standing but shouldn't have been. Her right leg was twisted at an impossible angle, and bone was poking through torn skin. Half of her face was so mangled he could hardly tell she was human, and the one eye James could see was pale and lifeless. She slowly started limping towards him, dragging her broken leg and groaning, reaching for him. Then the smell hit him—rotting meat. She smelled... *dead.*

"What the hell!" James said, drawing his handgun and taking a few quick steps back to join his brother.

"She isn't what I think she is... is she?" Connor asked.

Her groans intensified as she began picking up speed.

"She can't be, can she?" James asked.

"Stop, or we'll shoot!" Connor yelled, then turned to his brother and asked, "What do we do?"

"Let's drop back and figure it out. She's not coming too fast."

They backed up while keeping their guns trained on her. Clearly she should be dead—they could see that—somehow she wasn't. But she wasn't exactly alive either.

"She's a... *zombie*," James said. "I mean, look at her wounds. She should be dead right now."

"Then I guess it's time to shoot her. I mean it. Shoot *it*," Connor said.

He'd come to terms with what she—what it—was, and he was ready to deal with it. Moving his sights from her chest to her uninjured leg, he fired. Her knee shattered and she crumpled to the ground, but she kept coming, dragging her body and useless legs behind her.

"This is unreal," James said.

Connor aimed his gun at her chest and squeezed the trigger. The bullet flew out of the gun, blowing a hole in her heart. Her body shuddered with the impact but she kept coming. Finally, he aimed at her head, ready to end this. His left index finger squeezed the trigger, and her head jerked back. She fell onto her face, unmoving, blood slowly pooling on the blacktop. He lowered his gun, feeling a mix of emotions, but he pushed all those away. He would deal with them later. Right now they needed to survive.

James shook his head. "She *was* a zombie! This is crazy. It's actually happening—the zombie apocalypse."

"You'd better get used to it 'cause we're gonna be facing a lot more. And I don't want you to freeze when I think you have my back," Connor said a little harshly.

His words woke James up. "Don't worry. I would never hesitate to pull the trigger; you know that. I have your back, bro, against a person *or* a zombie." He put his hand on his brother's shoulder. "You did what you had to. Now let's get out of here."

Connor sighed. His older brother knew him so well, and with just those few words he had eased most of his doubts. They quickly walked back to the truck, keeping their guns at the ready. Jumping in, James made a sharp U-turn, leaving the carnage behind. Connor reached into the backseat and pulled his AR out of the case and loaded a thirty-round magazine.

He chambered a round and smiled at his brother, "At least we have a plan for this, right bro?"

James couldn't help but smile in return. "Yeah, we do."

It was true; they had created a farfetched plan for this, though neither thought they would actually use it one day. It had just been a joke. But now it was real, and they would put their plan into action.

It was a simple plan, really. They would gather their remaining family, maybe a couple of close friends, and head to their remote lodge in Alaska. There, they had everything they needed to be self-sufficient, with occasional supply trips into town using the bush plane Connor flew. The remoteness of the location would keep them safe from most of the zombies, and they would be able to live a somewhat normal life again, assuming everything went according to the plan, though it rarely did.

Once on I-94 they knew for sure. This was real. Abandoned cars were scattered on both sides of the interstate, accompanied by a few bodies and, every once in a while, a walking corpse. As such, the drive home took a little longer than usual. Each absorbed in their own thoughts, they drove in silence all the way to the dirt road that led to their house.

"So, how do you think it spreads? It has to be airborne, right? How else would it get to Cowtown?" James asked.

"Your guess is as good as mine. We must've missed a lot in the last couple days. I hope the internet and cell towers still work." Then it hit him. Their parents weren't at home safe and sound. They were hundreds of miles away in Nebraska, visiting family. "We need to get home! Quick!"

"On it!" James stepped on the gas, and the truck sped off down the dirt road.

Arriving at the house, James ran inside while Connor unloaded the truck, putting everything on the porch. Inside, James took a deep breath and said a quick prayer before picking his cell phone up off the desk. He turned it on and waited while it acquired a signal. Once it found service, he quickly dialed his mom's cell number and waited. The power worked and there was still cell coverage, but how long would that last?

"Oh, thank God you're okay! We've been so worried. We called the house earlier. We didn't know if you boys were still at the ranch or if something had happened," his mom, Diana, said.

"We're good," James said, "We were at the ranch the whole weekend. We didn't know anything was wrong until today. We need to be filled in, and fast."

"The truth came out the day you boys left. The government announced the outbreak of a deadly infection. It started in the towns where the blackouts took place and they tried to contain it there but failed. It hit *all* the major cities yesterday, and nothing has been heard from them since. It's just like all the zombie movies you boys watch, you get bitten and you turn. The government says everyone needs to barricade their house and stay indoors."

"Damn, this is worse than I thought. Are you guys safe?"

"Yes, honey. No one in town has turned yet and we are barricaded in. We'll be okay. Plus, God is watching over us."

"Good. You guys need to hold tight. Connor is packing the truck, and we'll be leaving shortly. You need to get to a defensible spot, get enough supplies for a few days, and stay there! We'll be down as soon as we can. Then we'll pick you up and head to Alaska. You remember our apocalypse plan, right?"

She chuckled a little. "I remember, but I always thought you boys were silly for having it."

"So did we, until today. Either way, we're putting it into motion. You need to stay put and stay safe!"

"We will, James. Your dad wants to talk. I love you, Son. I'm praying for you boys."

"Thanks, Mom. I love you, too. We'll need all the prayers we can get if we're to survive this."

"Son, are you there?" Jack said after a brief pause. There was a strength and determination in his voice that always comforted James and gave him courage.

"Yes, Dad, I'm here. Are you really safe? What's the weapon situation?"

"Don't worry about us, Son. We have enough guns and ammo thanks to some of your great-uncles. We're safe and secure for now. The... whatever it is, hasn't hit us yet. We'll be fine. You just watch your brother's back, okay? I'm counting on you two."

"I will, Dad. We'll be okay. We're more prepared than most. I love you."

"I love you too, Son. Now remember, we are Anddersons. We never back down, and we never give up. Mess with the best, die like the rest."

That was exactly what James needed to hear. He wiped a tear from his eye and handed the phone to Connor, who had just walked in.

James stood there for a moment, visibly at ease. A great weight had been lifted, replaced by determination and a desire to survive. Their parents were safe for now. Mom was praying for them, and that meant she still had faith. *And if she does, so do I*, he thought. While he didn't know all the theological answers or reasons why God would allow this to happen, he did know a few things. The End Times were talked about in the Bible as a time when God would let evil reign for seven years, and the Four Horsemen would come and destroy a fourth of the population with—among other things—a plague. He didn't know if that was what this was, and he didn't care. He knew who his Savior was and where he and his family would go after all this. And even in this, he could feel deep in his heart that God was with him.

Quickly running into the basement, he got all the ammo he could in one trip, and headed back up the stairs and out onto the porch. He walked back in as his brother finished talking to their mom.

"I love you, too, and we'll call you soon," Connor said, hanging up the phone. "They're safe."

"Yes they are, and God is with them and us," James said, going to his brother and hugging him.

"Yes, he is, even in these times."

They broke the embrace and stood there, looking at one another. Connor grasped James's forearm. "And we also have each other. We'll always have each other. Brothers till we die."

"Amen to that, brother. Now let's get packed."

They spent the next half hour getting all their gear together.

Luckily, they were hunters and keen on buying ammo in bulk. Together they had thousands of rounds of .223/5.56, .45, .40 and 9mm, plus hundreds of rounds for their shotguns and rifles. They took their primary guns out and put them on the porch, then put the remaining in a duffle and threw it into the back of the truck. Once they had their food, water, ammo, bedding, clothes, backpacks, and miscellaneous gear in the bed, they packed the backseat.

Lying in the middle was James's Benelli semi-auto 12-gauge shotgun, his Kimber Mountain Ascent .280 rifle with a 4-16x44 Vortex scope and katana, along with Connor's 10-gauge pump-action shotgun, Remington .308 rifle with a 3-10x42 Leupold scope, and machete. Also in the backseat they had plenty of ammo for the guns, along with some food, water, and other miscellaneous gear they might need in a hurry.

"Well, I think we got it all," Connor said, looking at the loaded truck—a white Dodge RAM 1500 crew cab with a lift kit, brush guard, and matching topper.

"I think so, it's almost like we were already prepared for this," James chuckled.

"I guess we kind of were."

James picked up his AR and chambered a round, his brother doing the same.

"Hey, look at us," James said, pointing at their reflection in the glass screen door as they stood there, holding their ARs.

Connor wore his Kryptek camouflage shirt and pants, combat boots, black hat, aviator sunglasses, and Kimber 1911 handgun on his hip. He had on his tactical vest, which held three magazines for his handgun, six magazines for his AR, a KA-BAR knife, and a multi-tool. James wore his Kryptek camouflage shirt, hat, and pants, hiking boots, transition lens glasses, and Springfield XDM handgun on his hip. He had on his tactical vest with three magazines for his handgun, six magazines for his AR, a long-bladed hunting knife, and a multi-tool. They had attached the tactical flashlights to their ARs, which were now fully decked out.

"We look badass!" James said

"Yeah, we do."

"Well, let's lock and load then."

James climbed into the driver's seat and stuck his AR next to him, going through a mental checklist. With everything checked off, he said a quick prayer for protection and guidance. Connor went through the house one last time, making sure they hadn't forgotten anything.

"We're all good to go, bro. Let's hit the road," Connor said, getting into the truck and setting his AR next to him.

The brothers pulled away from their house and looked up the hill to their parent's house. The boys' house was old and poorly made but livable and the right price for the brothers. Their parent's house was brand new. They'd built it a couple of years ago, moving out of the old house and letting James and Connor buy it. The family had lived here for years, and now in the course of a single weekend, everything had changed. They looked at the two houses and rolling gumbo hills, knowing this would be the last time they ever laid eyes on it. Finally, they pulled away, heading down the driveway.

"Hey, Connor, put on some tunes."

"Are you kidding me right now? You actually remembered to bring your iPod?" Connor asked, reaching down to hook up the iPod and then flipping through it.

"Just because it's the end of the world doesn't mean we can't ride in style!"

They turned off the dirt road onto the highway.

After a few minutes James asked, "What's taking so long, bro? I'd like some music today."

"One sec. You'll thank me when I'm done."

Just then the music came on. It was *Back from the Dead* by Skillet. They started cracking up; it was just too ironic.

"Let me guess—a zombie playlist?"

"Close. It's our Apocalypse Road Trip playlist," Connor said as they continued to smile. "You know what? This isn't going to be *that* terrible. I mean, we're still alive, and so are our parents. We're armed to the teeth and have all the skills needed to survive. We can stay alive and start over. This doesn't have to be the end."

"You're very right, brother, and most importantly, we have each other. As long as we have that, we'll survive. Don't ever forget, we ride together."

"We die together."

"Badass brothers for life!" they said in unison as they sped down the highway to face the apocalypse.

2
BREAKING NEWS

Friday, day before the "official" outbreak

"If you're just now joining us, nothing has been heard from Hill City. A dozen Texas state troopers have gone in to help with the power outage and Texas governor, Henry Price, urges citizens not to worry. We—wait—" There was a brief pause then the news announcer continued. "I'm getting some new information here. Yes, it seems that Lufkin, Jasper, and Nacogdoches are also experiencing blackouts. We just—"

The radio cut off and Emmett stood up from the couch. He'd been hoping his gut feeling was wrong and that the murders had been nothing, but now he knew his fears were well founded. He thought back to his past employer and shook his head.

Their greed will be the death of us all, he thought as he opened a drawer and pulled out a Beretta M9 handgun.

He put on a shoulder holster, sliding the gun on one side and two magazines on the other. He then pulled out a tactical belt with another Beretta M9, six magazines of ammo, a tactical knife, and a few pouches. Putting the belt on, he walked over and looked in the mirror. He had short black hair, brown eyes, a scar on his left cheek, and features like a hawk. He was in great shape, which made it hard to tell he was forty-years-old. He wore a white t-shirt, loose fitting jeans, and combat boots. He put on his black cowboy hat and dark brown duster, which had an odd assortment of items in the pockets. Then he pulled two duffle bags out from under the bed and went outside.

He put the bags in the bed of his black, four-door, Ford F-450 Super Duty, but it wasn't a normal F-450. The year before, he'd put over three hundred thousand dollars of upgrades into it, making it a fortress on wheels. He'd upgraded the engine, tires, and suspension, and the inside was as tricked out as it could get. There were bars over the windows, including the windshield and topper windows, which were all made of bulletproof glass. The body of the truck was also bulletproof with extra plating welded on in strategic locations. Add to that the matching heavy-duty topper had a pivoting shooting bench welded to the roof and the heavy duty grill guard with a winch.

There was an assortment of canned and dried food and drinks under the backseat, and ammo was shoved into the pockets on the backs of his seat covers. In the middle of the backseat was a weapons rack with a semi-auto 12-gauge shotgun with a collapsible buttstock and flashlight, a 6.5 Creedmoor custom rifle with a 6-24x50 Vortex scope, an AK-47 with iron sights, an H&K MP5 submachine gun, and a Desert Eagle with extended magazine. They were all strapped down so they wouldn't move around but could be grabbed quickly. In the front passenger seat there was a sawed-off 10-gauge pump-action shotgun and a machete.

This would be an odd and expensive collection for the average Joe, but Emmett Wolfe was far from average. He had served in the Marines during his younger years. After the Corps, he went to work in private security, most recently for his father-in-law's corporation, LifeWork. He had been the head of security at their main plant until quitting because of something he'd discovered. That was over a year ago, and since then he'd spent his time preparing for an event he hoped would never take place. Through all this, he'd never thought it was possible that it would actually happen.

He checked the back of the truck, making sure the topper was secure. Then he checked the bed, which contained mattresses, sleeping bags, a tent, two duffle bags with guns and ammo, fuel cans, totes of food, and a bolted-down toolbox cabinet. Everything was in order, so he headed back inside to do one last walkthrough. He grabbed a duffle bag of clothes from the closet and his Colt M4 carbine rifle with a red dot sight, suppressor, and flashlight from beside the front door. He then shut the door and screwed four boards over it. The rest of the house was barricaded in similar fashion. He didn't plan on coming back here, but he was keeping it as an option.

The truck roared to life as he took off down the driveway, the afternoon sun high in the sky. When he arrived at the highway fifteen minutes later, he turned east towards his ex-wife's house. He needed to get there fast. Jane lived just outside of

Hill City and their daughter would be with her for summer break. Six hours later, he was approaching Hill City and had seen very little traffic for the last half hour. *Is it that bad already?* he thought.

Emmett turned onto his ex-wife's road and pulled into her driveway, noticing a body lying on the ground. He grabbed his 10-gauge and machete from the seat next to him, slipping it into a sheath on his left hip. He chambered a round into the 10-gauge and walked up to the body, nudging it with the barrel of his shotgun, but nothing happened. He carefully flipped it over with his boot to get a look at the face. It was male, approximately thirty-years-old. This was not his ex-wife's current husband, which meant they could still be alive, hopefully. Putting the shotgun to his shoulder, he walked towards the front door. When he arrived, he noticed it was cracked. He leaned against the wall, and taking his left hand off of the shotgun, he eased the door open.

There was a loud *bang*, and the door exploded in front of him. He quickly withdrew his hand and looked at the door, which now had a large hole in the center of it.

"Watch it, you moron! Do I look like one of them?" Emmett asked the unknown shooter.

"No... none of them could talk," a man's voice said from inside.

"Well, at least you're not completely brainless. I'm coming in, George. Don't shoot!"

He stepped from the wall and went through the front door. Inside was a hallway, and at the end of the hallway there was a makeshift barricade with a man standing behind it. George looked scared standing there with a shotgun at his shoulder. He had blood splattered on the front and sleeves of his jacket. Two bodies rested face-down on the floor in front of the barricade.

"Where're Jane and Alexis?" Emmett asked.

"They're behind me in the bathroom. Is that you Emmett? What's going on? Why do you look like you're ready for war?" George asked, lowering his shotgun.

"Yes, it's me you twit, and that's because I *am* ready for a war. I'll explain everything once we get to the truck."

He headed over to the barricade and vaulted over it, then opened the door on the left and Alexis, his twenty-year-old daughter, came running out.

"Dad!" she said, hugging him tightly. Behind her, Jane came out and stood next to George.

"Hey there, sweetie," Emmett said, "I've missed you. Come on, we need to get to the truck before more of them show up."

He'd started walking with his daughter toward the barricade when George groaned. Emmett spun around, looking more closely at one of the bloody spots on George's arm.

In a fraction of a second he had his gun up. "You were bitten?"

George took a step back, eyes wide. "Yeah. Why does that matter? It's just a bite."

"It's not just a bite," he said, looking at Jane. "It's how the infection spreads."

"Infection? What are you talking about?" Jane said, moving to George's side.

23

Emmett looked at his daughter and then looked back at George and Jane. He lowered his shotgun.

"The infection? It's just the end of the world as we know it and the reason why people are coming back from the dead. But don't worry. I'm not going to kill you—at least not yet. But if you start to change, I *will* end you. Now, let's go." He started down the hall again towards the truck.

George stood there, stunned, mouth agape.

"We can't leave yet! I have to pack!" Jane said.

Emmett was about to snap back a response but bit his tongue when he looked at his daughter's face.

"You have five minutes."

Emmett went around the house, collecting a few grocery bags of food and raiding the medicine cabinet, then went out to the garage. Finally, after thirty minutes, George and the girls came out of the house, each carrying a suitcase. Emmett took the suitcases, throwing them into the bed of the truck.

"George, you'll sit in the front with me. Jane and Alexis, you sit in the back. Let's get moving," he said as they got into the truck.

"Jeez, Dad, what're all these guns for?" Alexis asked, grabbing the MP5.

"Insurance… You remember how to use 'em?"

"Of course I do. You've had me shooting since I was twelve."

She took a closer look at the MP5. She knew how to use a firearm but had never used anything like this before. Her dad was very protective, and when she was old enough, he'd had her take self-defense classes and learn to shoot. At the time, she'd enjoyed it but didn't realize how beneficial it had been until she was mugged. Well, the perp had *tried* to mug her with a knife, but you know what they say... Even now she carried her compacted S&W .38 revolver in her purse.

"Good, just making sure." He smiled as he turned around and started the truck. "Buckle up."

They left the driveway and hit the main road. Emmett was glad for all the time he'd put into training his daughter, but he never would have imagined her training would be used for this.

Alexis took a few minutes to examine the MP5, finding the safety, figuring out how to chamber a round, ejecting the magazine, and getting the general feel of the gun. Jane sat there, staring at her husband as George began to take heavier and heavier breaths.

"George honey, are you feeling alright?" Jane asked, putting a hand on his shoulder.

"Yeah," he said coughing, "I feel fine. Just a little cough, must be getting a cold."

"Are you sure? You don't look too good," Alexis added.

"Will you just leave me alone. I'm fine!" George snapped.

Jane looked like she wanted to say more but didn't. She removed her hand from his shoulder and sat back looking worried

The sun began to set, casting long shadows on the road as George wheezed and coughed. It was getting worse by the second. Emmett pulled the truck off the road and jumped out. He walked around to the passenger side and jerked George out.

"Hey, what are you doing?" George asked in indignation.

He wheezed as he stood on shaky legs, a sheen of sweat coating his pale complexion.

"You're infected, and you'll turn anytime now," Emmett said, pulling the Beretta from his shoulder holster.

"How do you know that?" George asked, weakly pointing an accusing finger.

"I've seen it happen before."

"So you're going to kill me? Just like that?" George coughed again and looked down in horror. Blood was splattered on his hand and dripped from his mouth.

"Just like that," Emmett said, training his gun on George's forehead.

Jane came around the truck, running to George. "Stop it!" she yelled desperately as she went to stand in front of her husband. "You can't kill him!"

"Sure I can. It's either that or he'll die, turn into one of them, and kill us. And I'm not letting you decide that." He kept his gun pointed at George.

"Dad's right. Something's wrong with him," Alexis said from the backseat of the truck. "Just look at him. But maybe we can take him to a hospital. We don't have to kill him."

George bent over, coughing. Blood covered his hands and the ground below him. Jane looked at him, distressed, tears in her eyes as she tried to think of some way to help.

"He needs help! Can't you see that! We have to help him!"

George fell to the ground and started to spasm. Jane went down next to him, tears streaming freely down her face as she tried to hold him.

"Get back, now! He's turning!" But Jane didn't move, so he addressed his daughter. "Look away."

He had taken four steps towards them when George stopped coughing, stopped moving, stopped breathing. He lay there, dead.

"We need to go, now!" Emmett said, trying to pull Jane away from her husband's lifeless body.

"No…" Jane whispered as she stubbornly held on to him.

George opened his eyes.

But they weren't *his* eyes anymore. These eyes were bloodshot, grey, lifeless. He let out a groan and moved his hand towards Jane's face. She gasped, pulling away. There were bruises all over his body from where his blood veins had burst open under the skin.

"BACK! NOW!" This time she didn't resist as Emmett roughly hauled her away from the undead George.

"Honey, are you okay?" Jane asked George as Emmett let her go.

George cocked his head as he looked towards her, rising unsteadily to his feet. He growled and lunged for them but was stopped mid-lunge as the muzzle of Emmett's gun flashed in the gathering darkness and the bullet tore a hole through his head. His head jerked back and he fell, rolling into a ditch on the side of the road.

"NO!" Jane screamed as she tried to run to him, but Emmett grabbed ahold of her. "You bastard!" She hit him, trying to get loose.

"Alexis, come get your mom and get her back into the truck, now!" He handed Jane to Alexis, and then he went down to the ditch.

A second gunshot could be heard over Jane's screams for her husband. He rolled George over with his foot. There was a hole in his forehead, and half his face was missing.

"Just like that," Emmett said. He turned around and walked back to the truck, climbing in and speeding off down the road with one less passenger.

Jane was crying in the backseat with her head in her hands.

"I'm so sorry mom," Alexis said trying to comfort her mother. She reached over and gently laid her hand on her mother's shoulder.

"Are we going to Dallas, where we're safe from this... infection?" Alexis asked.

"No, we're going north. It won't be long before this spreads to the bigger cities," he said as he topped out at seventy miles an hour, heading west to the interstate.

As they hit I-45 an hour later, they had passed no one on the road. But now they began to see the headlights of traffic. Emmett turned on the radio to hear a series of three beeps followed by a prolonged beep.

"This is the Emergency Alert System. This is not a test. There have been major power outages all over Texas and we urge citizens to stay indoors—" The broadcast cut off as Emmett changed the radio to a classic rock station.

Jane had stopped crying and was looking out the window with a blank expression.

"Dad, what's going on?"

"Something really bad, honey, and it's just beginning."

3
CLOSE CALL

The crosshairs of the scope settled on the zombie's head as it stared blankly through the window of the sporting goods store.

"They're everywhere," Connor whispered to his brother who was lying next to him with a pair of 10x42 Vortex binoculars in hand.

"Yes, they are, and I think it's just recently been overrun," James said as he took in the carnage. "There's no way we can drive in there with that horde by the grocery store. They'd be on us in no time. We'll have to sneak in."

This used to be a peaceful town full of good people. Now it was a bloody shell of what it had once been. He stood up and walked to the back of his truck parked in the middle of the overpass outside of town.

"Well, we have a choice to make. Do we want to go in and get supplies from the sporting goods store? Or play it safe and take our chances with the next town?" Connor asked as he stood up and walked over to the truck, setting his .308 rifle in the backseat and taking out his AR.

"I think we can get in and out, no problem, plus there could be survivors that need help," James said standing also. He set down his binoculars and swung his AR from his back.

"James, come on, bro. There *are* going to be survivors and they *will* need help. But we can't go into every overrun town just to save a few people. I want to help too, you know that, but we can't save everyone."

James was about to respond, but stopped himself and thought about it. In the end, he knew his brother was right. They couldn't save everyone. He checked his gear, both of them understanding that they were going in.

"They could have suppressors," James said as he finished throwing a few freeze-dried meals, water, and some boxes of ammo into his Kryptek hunting backpack.

"That would be ideal. More ammo and spare guns would be nice, too," Connor said as he did the same thing. "We'll only grab what we need. Let's hope no one else got to it first."

Connor grabbed his machete from the front passenger seat, and James grabbed his katana from the backseat, slipping the sheath into the back of his tactical vest.

"Switching to melee weapons," James said, cracking a smile.

They burst into laughter but quieted almost instantly, remembering all the zombies a few hundred yards away. However, they continued to chuckle softly as they started down the ramp into Miles, Montana.

Coming to the first gas station, they ducked behind it. Most of the zombies were clustered around the grocery store which sat behind the sporting goods store. The brothers were about six hundred yards from their target, with a couple dozen zombies between them and it.

James came to a halt before rounding the corner as he heard noises coming from the other side. He took point with his katana at the ready, AR slung at his side, and peeked around the corner. Ten feet away, kneeling over a gutted corpse, were two zombies munching away on the entrails. He moved back around the corner and held up two fingers.

Connor nodded.

James glided around the corner, his brother coming up beside him on the right. They quickly crept up to the zombies, which took no notice of them as they ate on a fresh meal. James brought his katana down on the one on the left as Connor brought his machete down on the other one. The zombies fell forward as the brothers pulled their weapons from their heads. Flipping the bodies over, they looked at them.

They were zombies alright, with grey lifeless eyes, gaping wounds, and intense bruising under the skin. The brothers looked at each other. These were the first they had killed and inspected afterwards. The zombies were beyond saving, and they knew that, but looking at them there was no doubt they had once been human. James felt a slight twinge of guilt but quickly dismissed it. They were zombies, and it was time to do whatever was necessary to survive. It had come to a point in the world where it was either kill or be eaten.

Moving on, they slipped around the back of the casino, encountering no zombies as they moved to the far edge. Looking around the corner at the street before them, they saw that there was no cover until the fast food restaurant on the other side. Ten zombies were shambling around in the street between them and where they needed to go. The brothers looked at each other and silently nodded. They knew what needed to be done.

Breaking from cover, they ran at the two nearest zombies. Their weapons came into contact with the zombies' heads and they fell to the ground, blood seeping from the wounds. The rest of the zombies in the street noticed the brothers and started walking towards them. They stood, back-to-back, waiting for the zombies to close in. The first one came at Connor, who took three steps forward and swung at its head, the machete sinking in a few inches. He yanked his machete from the zombie's head, and as it fell, he took three steps back to rejoin his brother.

James took a few steps forward and swung the katana, cutting a zombie's head clean off. He was surprised at how sharp the blade was as the headless body fell to the ground, another zombie taking its place. He quickly swung again, his katana taking the zombie in the side of the head as Connor's machete sank into a zombie's face. Now they were surrounded by four zombies, all of them coming at once. They slashed and stabbed, and when they were finished, there was a small pile of bodies around them. Looking at each other and their blood-covered blades, they smiled.

"Is it wrong that I enjoy this?" Connor asked as they ran across the street.

"Not at all. I do too, a little," James said as he wiped the blood from his katana. "But then again, brother, we were always a little different."

"That's true," Connor said, chuckling.

Their weirdness would be what would help them survive this horror. They moved to the back of the building, entering the alley. Two blocks down they spied the back door to the sporting goods store.

"It looks clear," Connor whispered to his brother.

"Let's go."

They took off across the alleyway to the back of the building, reaching the back door and glancing around, seeing nothing. Checking the door, they found it unlocked.

"Looks like they forgot to lock it in all the hurry," James said.

"Lucky for us," Connor said as he took point, James opening the door for him.

Connor entered the store with his brother following behind, covering his six. They swept left and right, but the back room was empty.

"Be alert. They could be anywhere," Connor whispered.

They moved through the room, their heads on a swivel, and arrived at the door leading to the shopping floor. Peeking through the small window set into the door, Connor saw two zombies staggering around. He looked at his brother and held up two fingers. They crept through the door and headed towards the zombies, their melee weapons at the ready. The zombies took notice as the door shut behind them, but it was too late, and their bodies dropped to the floor seconds later. The brothers quickly scanned for more, but finding the room apparently clear, they headed straight for the gun counter where they let out a collective groan.

"Looks like we weren't the only ones with this idea," James said, looking at the empty gun rack and shelves. He hopped over the counter and started to scavenge around behind it, looking for anything useful. Meanwhile, Connor was taking all the ammo they could use, which wasn't much, and shoving it into his backpack.

"Score!" James said as he picked up a box and set it on the counter. It was a suppressor for a .22 rifle. "There are more down here. We just need to find the right ones for our ARs."

After a minute of digging around, they were able to find four suppressors that fit their ARs, along with a few for various handguns and rifles. They unscrewed the birdcages off the end of their barrels, replacing them with the suppressors, and then shoved the remaining suppressors into their packs.

"Now that's more like it," Connor said, inspecting his newly accessorized AR-15.

"You like your new look?" James whispered to his AR, Victoria. He looked up at his brother, who was shaking his head, "What? You know she looks sexy."

James winked and Connor chuckled, then went back to collecting the few boxes of ammo scattered on the floor. James went throughout the store looking for anything useful. He came back with half a dozen tactical tomahawks and six sets of two-way radios.

"These may come in handy," James said, giving his brother a tomahawk.

"Ooh, but it's not Christmas yet!" Connor said with a gleam in his eye as he looked at the fierce weapon.

They each attached a tomahawk to their belts using the accompanying sheaves. Connor pulled his out of its sheath, and the metal snaps easily came undone. He had the weapon ready in one smooth motion.

Connor smiled and looked at his brother. "Thanks for the new toy, bro."

"Anytime."

James put the rest of the tomahawks and radios into his pack and went over to the wall he'd seen the freeze-dried meals on. He grabbed a bunch, along with a few camping stoves and small propane canisters. Connor finished collecting the boxes of ammo and grabbed each of them a camouflage yeti suit. His brother gave him a look.

"What? You never know when we may be hiding in a forest. I don't think the only thing we'll have to worry about is brainless zombies. Even during a disaster like this there are still evil people and—even more concerning—desperate people."

James had been thinking about that, too. Before all this was over, zombies wouldn't be the only thing they would have to kill. That thought didn't sit well with him, but he let it go for now and looked around. They had collected all they needed from here.

"You ready?" James asked, hoisting his pack onto his back.

He regarded his brother, standing there with his pack on, AR at his left side, tomahawk on his hip, holding a bloody machete in his hand, and dressed in his Kryptek Highlander camouflage. They must look formidable to anyone thinking of confronting them. *Good*, James thought, *that might discourage anyone from messing with us.*

"Let's do this," Connor said, moving to the back door. He signaled to his brother, who opened the door.

They exited the store into the alley and started back the way they'd come. Arriving at the street, they looked to their left. The horde of zombies was still clustered around the grocery store. *There must be hundreds of them!* James thought, knowing right away that something was different. The zombies seemed in a frenzy to get at something in the parking lot. Suddenly, a vehicle revved up, and they saw a blue car burst out of the horde and speed across the parking lot.

They looked at each other and quickly attached one another's melee weapons to the outside of their packs, then brought their ARs to their shoulders. The car sped around an overturned semi, only to unexpectedly collide with a zombie. The driver swerved as the windshield wipers failed to get the blood off the glass, and the car crashed into a light pole at the edge of the parking lot. Three figures stumbled out and began staggering away from the horde of encroaching zombies. One of the figures was clearly a male, while the other two looked female. None of them were armed.

The brothers assessed the situation.

"We have to try," James said to his brother, who nodded in agreement. They started off at a swift pace towards the three people.

"Hey! Over here! Help us!" the man yelled, waving his arm as he supported one of the women, who had an injured leg. The brothers were twenty yards from the trio, who were thirty yards from the lead zombies in pursuit of them.

"Head to the overpass. We have our truck parked just outside of town," James said when he made it to the group.

The man was Native American and had his long black hair in a ponytail. The woman he was supporting had short-cropped, multicolored hair, and her leg was clearly broken. The other woman was short and had long blonde hair in a messy jumble. They all appeared to be in their late twenties and were looking around in wide-eyed desperation.

"Go now!" James said when the trio slowed, having reached the brothers.

Connor was already past them when James got to the back of the group and took aim at the nearest zombie. Connor was the first to open fire, his shot taking the lead zombie in the head and dropping it to the ground. Another zombie fell with a hole in its head as Connor acquired his next target and squeezed the trigger. They were in perfect harmony. While one brother shot, the other acquired another target. They didn't "spray and pray" like in all the movies. They took their time and made quick headshots. Considering the range and the optics they had, it was hard to miss, although they still did a few times.

After a few seconds there were corpses scattered around the parking lot, tripping up some of the other zombies. James glanced over his shoulder to see where the group was and saw they were making good progress, turning into the alley behind the casino.

"Let's move," James said.

Connor fired one last shot, then got up and sprinted past James, tapping him on the shoulder as he ran by. James turned around and followed his brother towards the trio as they disappeared into the alley.

As the brothers rounded the corner, they saw the man trying to fend off a zombie with a trash can. Connor came to a stop and fired, and the zombie crumpled to the ground. The man glanced at them.

James passed them, taking point, "Come on!"

The man helped the woman with the broken leg up from the ground and they started off again, Connor bringing up the rear. They made it through the alley to the gas station at the edge of town without seeing any zombies. But when they stopped in the alley and James looked around the corner, he saw a horde of them between the gas station and the ramp leading out of town.

Connor joined his brother at the head of the group. "We can't stop for too long or they'll catch us."

"We have a bigger problem," James said, nodding to the corner of the building. Connor poked his head out and cursed under his breath.

"Talk about a rock and a hard place," he said, pulling his head back. "What's our next move?"

James assessed the group. The man was out of breath from supporting the woman with the broken leg, who couldn't move on her own. The only one who appeared to be able to move quickly was the short blonde woman.

"Okay," James said, sighing, "You and I go out and distract them while they go around to the ramp. Then we'll follow and meet at the truck. That's all I got."

"It'll have to work," the man said, looking back at the approaching horde coming into the alley behind them. "Here they come."

"We'll go first. Wait for us to start shooting and then run as fast as you can. Stay tight to cover and try not to attract attention. You'll have to be quick," James said as they switched out their magazines, replacing the partials with full ones.

James looked to his brother, took a deep breath, and then nodded.

The brothers burst around the corner, making it as far as the pumps before the zombies saw them. The horde started towards them, and they opened fire as they moved in a crouch. They made it around the horde with only a few yards between them and the closest zombies. In fifteen seconds, a dozen zombies were on the ground, and the trio began to move towards the ramp. Most of the zombies were intent on the brothers, and the group passed by the bulk of the horde without any trouble. The brothers backed up slowly towards the ramp, firing as they went.

A scream pierced the groans of the undead.

James and Connor glanced behind them in the direction of the noise and saw the man being taken down by a zombie. The woman with the broken leg screamed while trying to crawl away, and the blonde woman had picked up a small pole, using it as a weapon against the horde that was surrounding them. James didn't need to confer with his brother to know what to do. He took off running towards the group as Connor aimed at the zombie on top of the man sixty yards away.

As James ran, he heard a shot, and the zombie on top of the man jerked its head, blood spraying over the woman trying to crawl away. Connor was firing as fast as he could, but the zombies were closing in on her. James was still too far away to help and knew that if he stopped to open fire he wouldn't be able to make a difference in time to save her, so he ran faster.

The first zombie fell over the crawling woman, and her screams changed pitch to the most bone-chilling sound James had ever heard as three more zombies fell over her. A second later her screams were cut short as a shot rang out. *Was that a coincidence, or did Connor just...*

The thought was pushed from his mind as he remembered the last survivor. She was fending off a zombie that was blocking her way to the ramp. The ones behind her were temporarily preoccupied with the fresh meals and paid her no heed, but as James went around the feeding zombies, they looked up— fresh blood covering their faces—and started towards him. He arrived at the woman's side just as she bashed a zombie in the head and it fell to the ground.

"Stay with me and cover my back," James said as he turned around, ready to take out the small group coming towards him.

He took aim and the zombies started to drop like flies. He could see his brother in the distance as he came running towards them, zombies close on his heels. James switched targets to the zombie closest to Connor, and it fell to the ground, sporting a new hole in its head. He was already onto the next one, dropping it soon after. A few seconds later he had a good distance established between the zombies and his brother, and he went back to shooting the ones that were closing in on him and the woman. He took out the last three and cursed under his breath. The horde was almost on them. He opened fire again and was relieved a second later when Connor ran past him.

"Get her out of here. I'll cover!" Connor shouted as he turned around and took aim at the oncoming horde. James grabbed the woman by the arm and they ran towards the ramp.

Connor squeezed the trigger, and a zombie fell, dead. He squeezed again. *Click.* It was empty! He hadn't been counting his shots like he should've been. He dropped his AR, which swung to his side on the sling, and quickly drew his handgun, taking aim at the zombies now only a couple of yards away and closing in.

James arrived at the ramp and saw it was clear of any zombies. He quickly turned around and noticed that his brother was almost overrun.

"Come on, Connor!" James shouted, stopping just long enough to kill the two closest zombies and then continuing on his way, following the woman to the top.

Connor shot once more, and the slide stayed open on his handgun, indicating it was empty. He turned around and sprinted towards his brother as he quickly ejected the spent magazine and slapped in a new one.

James arrived at the top of the overpass and saw his truck sitting there. It was the best sight he had ever seen.

"Jump in the backseat!" he told the woman as he hopped in.

By the time he had the truck started and in gear, Connor was jumping in.

"Let's roll!" Connor said as he grabbed the shotgun from the passenger seat and stuck the barrel out the window.

James stomped on the gas and the truck took off, the force pushing them into the backs of their seats. They flew past as the horde made it onto the overpass.

Connor pulled the shotgun back in and rolled up his window. "Well, that was close."

4
REVELATIONS

Saturday, day of the outbreak

"Can we stop soon?" Alexis asked. Her legs ached from sitting in the truck for so long. They'd had to take several detours to avoid infected cities but they were finally in Oklahoma.

Jane still hadn't spoken since the incident with George the night before.

"I need to find somewhere to fuel up. Then we can stop," Emmett said.

They continued driving until he saw a sign for Hersham, Oklahoma. He'd been there before, and it would be a perfect place to fuel up.

They rolled to a stop in the middle of the highway, looking at the town. Emmett pulled a pair of 8x32 Leupold binoculars from the glove box and peered through them, knowing right away the town had been infected. There were abandoned cars, bodies strewn about, smoke rising into the sky, and the infected milling around.

"Alexis, Jane, stay in the truck no matter what. I'll clear the station and then you can come out," he said as they pulled into the fuel station on the outskirts of town.

He counted three infected around the station, and he drew his Beretta, pulling a suppressor out of his duster lying on the passenger seat. Screwing the suppressor on, he opened the door and stepped out. The infected, attracted to the noise of the truck pulling up, shambled toward him.

The nearest infected was ten yards out as Emmett took aim. It fell to the ground. The other two took no notice and continued at him, but they soon joined the first one on the ground, each sporting a 9mm-sized hole in their heads. Looking around for more threats and finding none, he grabbed the fuel nozzle, inserted it into his tank, and squeezed the lever, but nothing came out. He shook his head as he read the sign: Prepay or Credit Card Only.

Alexis rolled down the window. "Are they… *dead*?"

"They are now," he replied.

"Good. I really need to use the restroom."

"You can come in with me. I have to go in anyway. But first, I have a surprise for you." He walked to the back of the truck and retrieved a box from inside. "This is for you."

Alexis took the box and opened it, withdrawing a beautiful handgun. It was a Walther P99, painted in a purple and black camouflage. She looked at the gun in awe. It was the same kind she always shot at the range, and it fit her perfectly.

"Thank you so much!" she said, giving her dad a hug. She stepped back, looking up into her father's eyes and seeing a strength she knew would never fail.

"You're very welcome, honey. This goes with it," he said, handing her a tactical belt with a holster for her gun, a suppressor, three extra magazines, a multi-tool, and a knife. She put the belt on.

"I love it, Dad."

"I knew you would. Now, keep it with you at all times."

"I will," she said, sliding her handgun into the holster.

He then handed her a Benelli M4 12-gauge pump-action shotgun with a collapsible buttstock, pistol grip, and flashlight on the front.

"There, now you're properly outfitted. The main thing you need to remember is to shoot them in the head. That's the only way to put them down for good. You can do this, honey. I know you can."

He walked to the passenger seat where his suppressed M4 carbine awaited him.

Alexis looked down at the shotgun in her hands. Her dad believed in her, but she wasn't sure she believed in herself.

"Let's go. Stay behind me and stay alert. Jane, we'll be back," Emmett said as he moved toward the door of the fuel station, M4 at his shoulder.

Alexis followed behind him with the shotgun ready. As they walked forward, she kept close to her dad and looked around for any movement, remembering the training he'd given her.

Emmett reached the door and looked through the window. He saw a body on the floor, but there was enough blood for two or three. Half of the shelves had fallen over, and all of the merchandise was scattered around the floor. To the left was a counter with the registers where he would need to turn the pumps on. He turned to Alexis, who was also looking through the big glass window.

"Remember what I told you—aim for the head, and don't get bitten," Emmett said.

"I'm ready," she said, even though she didn't feel it.

She turned back to look through the window one last time at the horror inside. A bloody hand smacked against the other side of the glass. She jumped back, brought her shotgun up and pulled the trigger, but the shotgun didn't fire. She'd forgotten to chamber a round!

Her dad pushed through the door, already aiming down and to the left. Taking one look at the eyes, he fired. The infected collapsed to the floor.

Alexis stood there, looking at the bloody handprint on the glass. *This is more than I can handle . . . No, you can't think like that. You can do this,* she thought. She pumped the shotgun, chambering a round, and followed her dad through the door.

Emmett walked over to the body and put another round in its head for good measure. Then he went around to the counter, keeping his eyes peeled for movement. Glancing over the counter, he saw a body lying face down. It began to move, and he shot it twice in the head. He hadn't needed to check the eyes, knowing by the look and smell that it was an infected. He hopped over the counter and hit the button on the register, authorizing all the pumps.

"I'm good to go," he said to his daughter, who was standing on the other side of the counter, keeping watch. "I'll clear the rest of the station and then you can use the restroom. Get behind the counter and make sure nothing gets past me."

She nodded.

He moved down the aisle, reaching a body lying on the floor. He put a round in its head and went to the back door. He eased the door open and moved into the hallway. There were three doors. He swung the M4 onto his back and drew his Beretta. Checking the first door, he found it was locked, so he moved on to the next one. It was the women's restroom. He entered, Beretta up to his chest as he swept into the room. Ironically, the restroom was cleaner than the rest of the station, considering there was neither blood nor bodies. He cleared both stalls and went back out to the hallway, then entered the men's restroom. This one did have blood on the floor and a half-eaten body rested in the corner. He walked up to it. Half its head was missing, so he didn't waste a round. He cleared the stall and left the restroom.

"The restrooms are clear. Use the women's. It's clean," he told Alexis as he moved past her to the front door. As he walked out, he checked the surrounding area, finding it clear. He took the nozzle off and pressed the lever, it worked this time. He began to fuel up the truck.

Alexis was alone in the station now, and she certainly felt alone. Her dad was just outside and wouldn't have left if he hadn't thought it was absolutely safe, but that did little to alleviate her fear and she had to use all of her determination just to move from behind the counter. She walked to the back door and eased it open with the tip of her shotgun. There was nothing there, so she moved to the women's restroom. Even though she knew it was safe, her hands still shook as she opened the door. She walked inside, quickly looking around and keeping the shotgun pointed ahead. She didn't relax until she had checked both stalls.

Meanwhile, Emmett heard the lever click, indicating the tank was full, so he topped it off and hung up the nozzle. He knew it would be hard for his daughter, leaving her alone in there, but she needed to get used to it. He wouldn't always be around to protect her, and if she wanted to survive, she would need to toughen up. Alexis exited the station, walking confidently towards the truck, and he smiled to himself. *She'll do just fine.*

"Jane, do you need to use the restroom?" he asked through the open window. She answered him with a hateful look, the grief plain in her eyes.

Alexis walked up and opened the back door. "I'll take you, Mom. The restroom is actually very clean." She helped her mom out of the truck and they walked inside.

Emmett stood by the pump, wondering if they needed any supplies from the station. Walking back inside, he grabbed some cold drinks and snacks for the girls. He had plenty of survival food, but he thought they'd like this better.

He was leaning against the truck, reloading a thirty-round magazine, when the girls came out. It had taken them over twenty minutes, and five new corpses accompanied the original three. It looked like Jane and Alexis had been crying, and he guessed they'd had a "girl talk" while in there. Girls loved to use the bathroom for that sort of thing.

"Are you two ready? I have some snacks inside," he said as he finished reloading his magazine, slamming it into the M4.

"Yes," Jane replied, venom dripping from her voice.

At least this was an improvement, considering she wouldn't talk to him before. They loaded into the truck and left the gas station behind.

Driving through the day, they'd stopped several times for gas. They were south of Kansas City on I-49. Emmett had to drive more cautiously now as abandoned and crashed vehicles littered the interstate. They'd been seeing quite a bit of traffic going both ways with people driving erratically. More than once they'd watched as a vehicle swerved and crashed into the ditch or another vehicle. They didn't stop to see what had happened; he had a pretty good idea.

"Can we stop for the night?" Jane asked.

He knew from experience that she didn't sleep well in a moving vehicle.

"Yeah, we just need to find a good spot," he replied.

"Dad, why are we going north?" Alexis asked, suppressing a yawn.

"I have a… fortified building up there, and it has everything we need. You'll even have your own room," he replied.

"You think of everything. But why north?"

"The infection doesn't do so well in the colder weather and neither do the infected."

"So…where *are* we going?" Alexis asked.

Looking in the rearview mirror, he could tell Jane wanted these questions answered too.

"Alaska. The farther north we get, the better."

"Wait. You show up, throw us in the truck, shoot my husband, and expect us to go all the way to Alaska with you?" Jane asked, furious.

"Would you rather I'd left you there in the capable hands of your ignorant husband?"

"You never liked him. You always wanted him dead!"

"No, I never did like him, but I wouldn't have wasted a good bullet on him if he hadn't been infected. But he was, so I did to him what I'll do to every infected I see. Get used to it, *dear*, because it's only going to get worse."

"Enough! Must you two always fight?" Alexis asked. She hated seeing her parents this way. She loved them both dearly, but they had some serious unresolved issues they needed to work through. "So why are we going all that way? I thought we were just leaving Texas, maybe to Montana at the farthest. Is it that serious?"

Emmett wanted to chuckle at that but stopped himself. They didn't know what he did, and he didn't expect them to understand.

"Yes, honey, it's very serious. Last we knew, it was just Texas, but the infection will spread. Within a couple days, the places infected will outnumber the ones not. In a couple weeks, we can expect the whole U.S. to be infected, if not all of North America. After that, who knows what'll happen."

It was silent for a few minutes.

"How do you know all this?" Jane asked, fuming.

He had been wondering when the questions would come to this one.

"You won't like the answer. But I'll tell you anyway as it'll be all over the news soon enough. Your father's company is involved. I discovered something while working security there— something that alarmed me and made me do some digging."

"You're a liar! He would never be involved in something like this! I can see now what happened between you two," Jane said, realizing that it had been more than just the divorce.

Albert, her father, and Emmett had always been close, but something had happened around the time of the divorce, and Emmett quitting had put them at odds.

"Believe what you want. You'll realize there's more to LifeWork than you think, a lot more," he said. "There's a rest area up ahead. We'll stop there for the night."

As he pulled off the exit he noticed a vehicle pulling back onto the interstate. Driving up to the rest stop, he had his choice of parking spots, so he pulled into the space right in front of the restrooms. Here, the street lights illuminated a good twenty yards in all directions.

"Now, honey, concerning your handgun, you need to be careful. Best to conceal it while in public, but make sure to keep it close. You never know who's infected."

Alexis threw on her jacket and got out of the truck, looking around nervously. Emmett got out and went towards the building. Inside, he cleared both restrooms. There was no blood or bodies. Alexis and Jane went into the restroom before bed while he unstuffed two of the three sleeping bags in the bed of the truck and laid each on a mattress. He threw the other one onto the roof of the topper next to the shooting bench. The girls came out and looked at the sleeping bags and mattresses.

"Is this for us?" Alexis asked, surprised.

"Of course," he said, enjoying her reaction. "I'll keep a watch from the roof. Just make sure all the windows are closed back there. You'll see that the tailgate and topper can be opened and closed from the inside."

After they climbed into the bed of the truck, he heard the latch lock and knew they were safely inside. He climbed onto the topper and crawled into his sleeping bag, his M4 within reach. He closed his eyes, going into a light sleep, and knew even the slightest sound would wake him.

Emmett woke up early the next morning, sore and stiff from sleeping on the hard surface. *I'm not as young as I once was*, he lamented to himself. He looked around at the rest area, and saw that it was empty, same as the night before. Taking care not to wake the girls, he grabbed his M4, climbed off the topper, and walked into the restroom where he splashed cold water on his face. When he left, he felt awake and ready for the day.

He knocked on the topper window. "Girls, it's time to get up," he said, receiving only a series of groans as a reply.

He grabbed his rifle from the weapons rack and climbed onto the roof again, where he sat resting his rifle on the bench. The girls got out of the truck and went straight into the restroom. They came out only a few minutes later, surprising him. He had lived with them for years and had never seen them get ready this fast. *I guess the apocalypse really does change people*, he thought.

They retrieved their things from the bed of the truck and hopped into the backseat. Jane immediately laid her head against the window and closed her eyes while Alexis rested her shotgun next to her and buckled up. He did one final scan, then climbed off the topper, stored the rifle on the rack, and got into the driver's seat. A minute later, they were back on the interstate, driving north toward the Land of the Midnight Sun.

5
A KILLER'S CONSCIENCE

"Yes, Mom, we'll be safe. We love you, and we'll call tomorrow," James said as he hung up and turned to his brother. "Mom and Dad are safe. They're holed up in a farmhouse out in the country. They were attacked by zombies this afternoon. Grandma and grandpa didn't make it; it's only them now. They barely made it out alive, and in their hurry, dad was only able to grab a hunting rifle."

James gazed out the window at the barren landscape of South Dakota as it passed by. They were dead. He'd known this would happen eventually, but now that they were actually gone, it made this whole "apocalypse" thing seem much more real.

After a few minutes of silence, Connor spoke. "I figured they wouldn't last long. Maybe this is for the best."

"I'm sorry to hear about your grandparents," Felicia said from the backseat.

She hadn't said much since they'd rescued her in Miles, but he couldn't blame her. She'd been the only one of her group to survive.

"Thanks," James said, taking his eyes off the road and glancing back, giving her a friendly smile.

He couldn't help his eyes lingering on her. She had long blonde hair pulled into a ponytail, striking blue eyes, and soft features. She was short, with an athletic build, and couldn't have stood much over five feet. However, the reason his eyes lingered was the fear in her eyes. There was hopelessness also, and he could tell she was having a hard time dealing with this.

"I'm sorry about your friends," James said, turning his attention back to the road.

Checking the gas gauge, he noticed they were at a quarter tank. They had only filled up once after Miles.

"It's okay. They weren't my friends, really. We went to the same college, but I hadn't known them till... this," she said, looking out the window.

"Do you want us to find you a vehicle at the next stop so you can head back to your family?" James asked. He knew he was taking a risk, asking about her family, but if she wanted to go back it was best to let her go as soon as possible.

"No..." she said, pausing. "My family's gone."

"I'm sorry to hear that."

"They've been gone for a few years now, and I don't really have anyone."

"Surely you have someone," Connor said, chiming in, "a strong, pretty girl like you."

James looked at his brother, shocked at how straightforward he'd been. Connor returned his look and shrugged, mouthing "apocalypse."

Felicia smiled a little. "Surprising, right? I was very close to my family, and after they passed in the same year as my best friend, I decided I didn't ever want to hurt like that again."

"Makes sense," Connor said, distracted.

He was no longer listening. His attention was on the car driving towards them on the highway. As it got closer, it began slowing down.

"Bro, you might want to check this out," Connor said, pointing.

The car drove across the line into their lane, where it stopped and four people got out. They were armed with a shotgun, two rifles, and a semi-auto rifle.

"I don't think they're friendly," James said as he eyed the people. "We may want to prepare ourselves."

"Already on it," Connor said.

He rolled down his window and stuck his .308 rifle out. James slowed the truck when they were two hundred yards away and pulled a little to the left to give his brother a steady rest on the side-view mirror.

"How's the shot?" James asked his brother as he watched the people start to walk towards them.

"Good," Connor responded, aiming through the ten-power scope.

"Who are you, and what do you want?" James yelled out his window as he leaned out, aiming with his AR.

"We're friends," the lead man said, smiling. There were three men and one woman. They looked disheveled, with spots of dirt and blood on their clothes.

"Stop there and we can talk," James said. He watched their casual movements as they continued forward, guns lowered.

"We shouldn't have to yell. We'll come to you," the leader said.

"I said stop there!" James yelled back.

When they didn't stop, Connor let a round fly right at their feet to accentuate the point. The group stopped, raising their guns. Connor already had another round in the chamber and was scoped on the leader. He would be the first to die.

"I told you to stop. We can talk from here. No need to get closer."

"What? You don't trust us?"

"Not at all," James said.

"We just wanted to see if you had any room for us to hop in," the leader said, his smile still plastered on his face. It unnerved James how much this man smiled. No one should smile while they were being shot at. The leader continued, "As you can see, our little car over there is not the best for running over zombies. But that truck of yours. . . damn, it looks good. You get it lifted?" They began to lower their guns as the leader continued talking.

"Yea—" James was cut off as two things happened at once.

First, he heard a shot echo through the truck as his brother fired. Second, the leader fired one shot before falling to the ground, blood spraying from his neck. The shot just missed the truck, whizzing by as James aimed at the other man with a rifle, who was shouldering his weapon as he sighted in on them. James fired when his crosshairs settled on the man's head, and the bullet struck the ground just to the man's right, but it was enough to make him flinch and miss his shot. James wasn't used to being shot at while he was trying to aim.

He heard his brother shoot again and saw the woman with the other rifle fall to the ground, blood staining her shirt. James got his target back in his scope and *squeezed* the trigger. His shot took the man in the shoulder as he was bringing the gun back to his eye from racking the bolt. The man dropped the rifle, his arm no longer able to support it, and had begun to pull out a handgun when James's third shot took him square in the chest.

In the span of a few seconds, three of the four lay on the ground, dead or dying. After shooting at the brothers a couple times, the man with the shotgun realized his firearm wasn't effective at that range. He sprinted in a crouch back toward their car. James sighted on him but hesitated. He was running away and wasn't a threat to them now. Most likely, he would get in the car and high-tail it out of here. But what if he didn't? What if he had a rifle in the car, or something worse? James was too late making up his mind as his brother's rifle barked and the man fell forward.

James looked around, noticing there were a few zombies heading towards them from some of the abandoned vehicles in the ditches. The noise of the gunfire must have drawn them.

Connor pulled the rifle back inside, opening the empty bolt, and began loading.

"Just another reason to load a bullet in the chamber when the mag's full," Connor said, as he finished and set the rifle in the backseat. "Let's roll up and get their guns."

James shook his head. He needed to wrap his mind around this or he would get them into trouble. He glanced at his brother.

"Sorry, bro," James said in a half whisper.

"I had him. No reason for you to waste ammo at that range," Connor said, a hard look in his eyes.

"Yeah, but—"

"We can talk about it later. Let's get those guns and get out of here."

James sighed and pulled the truck forward two hundred yards to the first three bodies. A zombie had already started to eat on one of the bodies and more were a hundred yards away. Connor hopped out of the truck, grabbing his machete and dropping the zombie with a blow to the head. He then stabbed the three bodies in the head and grabbed their firearms and all of the ammo they had, which wasn't much. He jumped back into the truck, throwing the guns into the backseat opposite Felicia, who sat there looking scared and unsure.

James pulled the truck forward and Connor got out again, grabbing the shotgun off the last man and walking the few yards to their car. Several zombies were gathered around it. Connor slashed the first one in the head, dropping it. James leaned on the side-view mirror with his suppressed AR and took out two zombies closing in on his brother, and Connor took care of the last two. James jumped out of the truck and shot a zombie heading their way. The zombies were scattered enough that they wouldn't overwhelm them anytime soon, so he walked up to his brother who was loading some items into a bag.

"Anything good?" James asked.

"Some ammo and a few other miscellaneous items," Connor said, pulling his head out of the backseat and zipping the bag shut. "Pop the trunk."

James went to the driver's door and did as he'd been asked.

"Bastards," Connor whispered.

James came around the side of the car and gasped. There was a woman in the trunk, tied up and bloody, and she looked to be in pretty bad shape. Connor felt for a pulse at her neck. Pulling his hand back, he shook his head and drew out his KA-BAR, gently shoving it into the back of the woman's neck at the base of her skull.

"No reason for her to come back like this," Connor said softly.

James was always amazed with his brother. He was a hard man who wouldn't hesitate to shoot an evil man in the back. But on the same coin, he would show compassion to a dead woman who had suffered.

"Let's go," James said, watching the growing swarm of zombies.

He raised his AR and sighted on the closest one, dropping it to the ground. Connor picked up the bag and went back to the truck. James followed and jumped in, set the AR next to him and drove around the car with the dead woman in the trunk as they continued on their way.

They'd been driving for a few minutes when Felicia finally spoke. "How...?"

They both shrugged.

"It was them or us," Connor said, "and I'm not ready to die yet. Are you?"

"No… but it was so easy for you," she said.

"Killing isn't the hard part. You just aim and squeeze the trigger. Killing a person is no different than killing an animal, especially when it comes to survival. No, the act of self-defense isn't a hard choice. Squeezing the trigger is easy. It's living with that choice afterwards that's hard," Connor said, some of the hardness leaving his eyes.

"But—" she began.

"You cannot hesitate in war, and make no mistake, this is a battlefield," Connor said, looking over at his brother.

James could feel his brother's eyes on him and knew what he was saying with that look. *Get it together, bro*.

James knew his brother was right. His hesitation would get them killed, and he couldn't do it again, not with a zombie or person. It was them against the world. He thought about the commandment, "Thou shalt not murder." How could he kill without murdering? He thought about all the soldiers fighting overseas. Were they murderers? No, he knew that wasn't true. They were in a physical *and* spiritual war against evil. But was this the same thing? His brother's last comment replayed in his head. "Make no mistake, this is a battlefield." If this was a war then he would have to man up and move forward. He *would not* let his hesitation be the end of them. He would just have to come to terms with what needed to be done.

64

James fueled the truck while Connor kept watch. The pump kicked off and he topped off the tank, then hung up the nozzle.

"We should gather all the food we can from inside," James said, walking around the front of the truck to join his brother.

"I need to use the restroom," Felicia said, getting out of the truck and stretching.

James watched her. She was pretty—not like an overdone hotness but the gentle type of cuteness he preferred.

"I can escort you," James said, walking over to her and smiling.

"Thanks," she said, giving him a small smile.

"You'd better take this," Connor said, offering her the 12-gauge semi-auto shotgun. "It's fully loaded. All you have to do is click the safety off and pull the trigger."

She took it and James showed her the safety and how to shoulder it. He nodded and Connor led the way to the gas station.

They reached the building and Connor stopped beside the door while James came up to it and nodded to his brother. Connor opened the door and James took a step inside, scanning the room. There was nothing he could see right away, but he could smell something rotten. Felicia and then his brother came in behind him.

"What *is* that?" Felicia asked, putting a hand up to block her nose.

"Rotting flesh," Connor said.

"Connor," James said, chastising.

"What? It's the truth," he said, glancing at Felicia who was growing pale. "Sorry, I meant to say… a field of roses."

James chuckled and Felicia smiled despite the situation. As they moved further into the room, the brothers swung their ARs to their sides and pulled out their tomahawks. They made it to the back of the room, finding nothing, and only had the restrooms to check.

"I'll get the men's. You get the women's," James told his brother.

"Yes! I have always wanted to go into a women's restroom," Connor said. James and Felicia gave him a look. "What? I'm curious. Do you have couches where you sit and talk, or vending machines, or…"

He trailed off as Felicia started laughing.

"Boys," she said.

"Let's just check these," James said, shaking his head.

He couldn't take his brother anywhere, even at the end of the world. James pushed into the men's restroom and noticed right away all the blood on the floor and walls and the chunks of flesh lying around the room. He searched around but didn't see a body, only pieces of one. Crouching down, he looked into the single stall. It was empty. Hearing a thud from the other side of the wall, he exited the restroom, quickly opening the door to the women's room and looking in. There was a body lying on the floor, blood leaking from its head. His brother came out of the second stall.

"Clear in here," Connor said as he walked past his brother and out the open door.

James grabbed the body by a leg and hauled it out of the restroom.

"There you go," he said to Felicia as she went inside.

James walked over to his brother who was searching the gas station for anything useful.

"I won't hesitate again," James said.

"I know, bro," Connor responded. "I have full confidence you would've done it. You just would've taken a little longer. I envy you sometimes, you know."

James looked at his brother in surprise.

"What? I do, I've been wondering..." Connor said, standing as he looked at his older brother. "It's easier for me to do all this, but is that really a good thing? Does my lack of hesitation mean I'm just as bad as them?"

"No, it means you're stronger in your resolve than I am. You have to remember, Connor, you were a marine. Yes, you never saw combat, but you had the mindset and were ready for war. You were ready to die and to kill for your family and country. This is no different. I've been thinking about it for the past few hours. What makes it murder?" James paused and noticed he had his brother's full attention. "I think I have an answer."

After a brief pause, Connor said, "And?"

"Think about it. God knows our hearts, minds, and souls. He knows everything about us, what we will do and what we could do. He knows *our hearts*, and that's the difference," James said, becoming animated. "We don't want to kill; we're driven to do it. But an evil man, he *wants* to kill. God looks at our hearts. It's that simple."

"That's what I'm afraid of," Connor said in a hushed voice.

"Brother, if you're asking these questions then your heart is *not* evil." James stopped talking as Felicia walked out of the restroom, looking refreshed.

"Much better," she said.

"Good," James said, looking at her and then around the room. "I guess we're done here. Nothing worth our time."

They left the gas station and climbed into the truck, taking off down the road.

"I'm sorry for how I acted earlier," Felicia said when they were back on the highway. "I was shocked. I've never seen anything like that before."

"It's okay," James said, "It was shocking for us, too. We're just better at hiding it. And Connor's right. If we hadn't killed them, they would've killed us, or worse. They had a woman tied up in their trunk. She was alive when they put her in there."

Felicia shook her head, "That's horrible. It amazes me what evil we're capable of."

The brothers nodded in agreement.

"So, what were you studying at Miles University?" James asked.

"Psychology. I'm fascinated with the human mind," she said, passion creeping into her voice. "What we as humans are capable of—the evil yes, but the good, too—it's intriguing. All the choices we make in our daily lives shape who we are and who we are to become. But what decides those choices? Are we predetermined to lean towards a certain choice? Or do we adapt to the outcomes of past choices? The same situation will affect people differently. Leaving a lasting impact on some while others are unaffected. It is all so fascinating!"

"This must be interesting for you then—what people are willing to do at the end of the world, what it'll drive some people to do, and the things we *must* do to survive," Connor said.

"Why yes, it does. I haven't been able to think about it much because I've just been trying to survive another day. But now that I have some time to think, it is interesting…" She pulled a small notebook out of her back pocket and began to write some notes down. "Yes, this should be interesting..." she mumbled to herself.

Connor noticed her write both their names down, followed by more notes in a smaller script he couldn't make out.

"Looks like we're her new experiment," Connor said, leaning over to whisper in his brother's ear.

James smiled and shook his head. "Shrinks."

They both shared a chuckle as Connor turned the stereo on and their Apocalypse Road Trip playlist began to play *Aim for the Head* by Creature Feature. The sun had set and the sky was beginning to darken around them.

Today was one hell of a first day, James thought as the truck's headlights illuminated the road ahead.

6
TRAPPED

Emmett cursed under his breath as he glanced around the corner, seeing the hundreds of infected that waited for them in the parking lot. He pulled his head back and turned, looking at the three women crouched behind him in the dead-end alley. Alexis looked at him expectantly, but he just shook his head.

"The way to the truck is blocked. We have to go back inside," he told them.

Jane sighed at the prospect of going back into the department store. Even now she could hear the groaning of the infected inside.

Emmett looked back and noticed the two younger women looking at him with a fire in their eyes. He couldn't help but feel proud of his daughter. She'd been through a lot in the last few days and yet she hadn't given up hope and had grown stronger from it. He looked at her crouched there. She looked fierce with her handgun in a holster on her right thigh, tactical belt around her waist, a machete in a sheath on her other hip, and her shotgun in her hands. He stared at her for a few moments, taking in the woman his daughter had

71

become. It almost brought him to tears. He was pulled from the moment by a voice.

"I'm sorry I got you into this mess," the third woman, Ana, said with a slight Russian accent.

She was in a disheveled state, with her auburn hair in a mess and her clothes torn and bloody, but she had determination in her eyes. She held his other Beretta—his hip holster was now empty—and she had a crowbar tucked into her belt.

"It isn't your fault," he said. "We chose to help. Now we need to go while we still have a chance."

He glanced over at Jane and noticed that the fire in her eyes was no longer there. It had died years ago. She held his AK-47 and had a large knife on her belt, not that she had used either yet. He tried to keep her towards the back, out of the fighting. Alexis and Ana nodded to him. *Time to get this done.*

He stood up and moved past the women, who followed him—Ana right behind, Jane in the middle and Alexis bringing up the rear. They made it back down the alley to the door they had barricaded with a dumpster. Even now, the infected were trying to claw their way through, and a few had their arms sticking through the crack in the door.

"I'll roll the dumpster away from the door a few inches. Alexis, Ana, you stab them through the crack. Jane, watch our backs and make sure none come down the alley."

Jane turned around, looking down the alley, rifle at her side. Ana stuck the Beretta in the back of her pants and Alexis set the shotgun down next to the door. They both pulled out their close-range weapons and positioned themselves next to the crack, causing the infected inside to go into a frenzy. Emmett swung his M4 onto his back and went over to the side of the dumpster with the locked wheels, then looked at the girls. They nodded and he kicked down on the locks, freeing the wheels. The dumpster slid away from the door, with the infected pushing from inside. He engaged the locks, but still the dumpster continued to slide until the door was halfway open.

The first infected pushed through the gap, leaving bits of flesh on the door and frame. Alexis took a step back, then plunged her machete through its brain as another came through. Ana stepped up and bashed the next one in the head with her crowbar, two more taking its place. Emmett quickly drew his Beretta and in two shots the infected fell dead, inches from the girls. Those two were replaced with two more as they kept coming through the partially open door. The girls took care of the next two and the two after that while Emmett kept his gun trained on the door in case things got out of hand.

Twenty infected lay dead outside the door as he pushed the dumpster away completely. The girls were ready in case something came through the door, but when it opened all the way, it revealed an empty room. Moving up next to the girls, he peered inside at the small room and hallway beyond that.

"We should be good for awhile. Most of the ones that were chasing us are dead now," Emmett said, glancing down.

Alexis grabbed her shotgun from the wall and took up her place in the back. They had established this order when they had come into the department store the first time. Actually, they had been forced to enter the store, which was connected to a mall.

While fueling up earlier, Emmett had seen Ana enter the mall with two men, chased by a horde of infected, and he'd decided to help. Emmett and Alexis had followed them inside, with Jane insisting that she come, too. When they found Ana, she was with only one of the men. The other had fallen. The newly formed group fought their way into a restroom, where they were trapped. They put their heads together and came up with a plan, and Emmett gave each of them a gun. Shooting their way out of the restroom, they made it into the mall, but they had been forced to enter the department store because of a horde chasing them. The other man with Ana had sacrificed himself so they could escape out the door they had just come back through.

Emmett crouched in the hallway, looking at all the hiding places the infected could be. It was dark inside, with the only light coming through the glass doorways and windows in the ceiling. He knew there were more infected between them and where they needed to go, but if they could just get through the mall, they would be able to come out only a few yards from the truck.

He looked back, holding a finger to his lips. They would need to be silent. The girls nodded and he began to move forward, the others trailing behind. Armed with his suppressed M4, Ana with her crowbar, Jane with the AK, and Alexis with her shotgun, they moved through the store. Sticking to the aisles where light was coming down from above; they arrived at the entrance that led to the rest of the mall. He signaled them to a stop by the door.

Looking back at Ana, he asked, "Do you know how to use a handgun?" He'd given her his Beretta already, but he'd had little time to see if she knew how to use it.

"Yes," she answered, the accent obvious in her voice. "My father taught me."

"Good. We'll try and move quietly, but if we start to get overwhelmed, we'll do away with stealth and get to the truck quickly. Clear?"

"Roger that," Alexis responded, checking the chamber of her shotgun.

"Yes," Ana answered, hefting the crowbar.

"Sure," Jane said, looking around nervously.

"Let's go then."

He opened the door and they left the store, heading into the large hallway with stores lining both sides. They went forward in a low crouch, trying to stay as quiet as possible but still moving with speed. They made it halfway to the 'T' at the end of the hall before seeing the first infected. It walked from around the left corner, sniffed the air, and looked at them with dead eyes. It let out a low groan and started shambling their way, followed by another one.

Emmett looked back, held up two fingers, and pointed to himself. He broke off from the rest of them, springing forward and swinging the M4 onto his back. Grabbing the machete at his side, he slashed one in the head and then stabbed the other in the face. They fell to the ground in a heap and he quickly looked around the corner the infected had come around. There were a bunch of infected in between them and where they needed to go. He motioned for the women to join him at the corner, and they slowly came forward, staying alert.

"Looks like we've got about twenty infected out there. We'll have to take care of them before we can get to the doors and the truck beyond that," Emmett said.

They all nodded, looking to him for a plan.

Alexis was at the back of the group as they moved around the corner. Her job was to back them up with the shotgun if things got out of hand. Her mother was back with her. Her dad and Ana would lead with their close-range weapons and take the infected out quietly. Alexis was on edge, but her dad hadn't led them wrong yet. Yes, they were in a bad situation because of coming in after Ana, but Alexis would have done the same in his position.

Her dad and Ana reached the first two infected as their lifeless eyes turned their way. They dropped them to the ground, moving on to the next ones. In this manner, they continued moving through the hall, slaying the infected, and had half of them down before the last ten took notice. Now the rest were all starting to slowly head toward them, their groans intensifying. Alexis knew this was bad. Any of the infected within hearing distance would hear those frenzied groans and know prey was close.

She kept an eye ahead while also watching behind and to the sides, and she was the first to see the horde of infected coming around the corner behind them. She whistled twice, keeping her eyes on the slowly advancing horde. A few more infected began to appear on all sides, coming out of the darkened stores. She whistled twice again, then again, alerting her dad that they were slowly being surrounded. She looked to the front and saw that her dad and Ana were surrounded by a small group of infected. She raised her shotgun to her shoulder, but after a look from her dad, she lowered it. She pushed her mom to move faster. They had to get to the front and help out.

Jane didn't want to be here—not in this mall and especially not with her ex-husband. He was such a pig. To think he had killed George in cold blood! Yes, she was beginning to realize George was turning and would be like the rest of these... *things*. But that didn't change the fact that Emmett had shot him, and she would never forgive him for that, whatever the reason.

Jane was so caught up in her thoughts that she failed to see the leg lying on the floor and she tripped, falling forward and letting go of the rifle in her hands in order to catch herself. She felt a crunch in her left wrist as it hit the floor and pain in her ankle as she fell. She looked down at her left hand as it hung there on the end of her arm, twisted at an odd angle, and she tried to get up and retrieve her rifle, but as she put weight on her right ankle, pain shot up her leg and she stifled a scream.

"Mom, are you okay?" Alexis asked, coming over to help her up. She had Jane's rifle in one hand, shotgun in the other. "We need to go! They're coming!"

Emmett ran back to them, covered in blood, his movements hurried.

"Give her to me and go with Ana," he said, picking Jane up. "And if we don't make it, go without us!"

Alexis looked like she was going to protest, but Emmett pushed her forward, giving her a look. She ran up to Ana, who was standing next to the doors that led outside.

Emmett and Jane began to move after the girls. Jane limped alongside her ex-husband, all her hate for him having vanished now that her survival was at hand. She made the mistake of looking back and let out a gasp as she saw that they were mere feet away from being overrun by the horde of infected. Luckily, they made it to the doors and pushed outside where Alexis was at the truck, beckoning to them. Ana was next to the doors they'd come through, ready with a long piece of metal, which she shoved through the handles as soon as they made it out. Then she ran to join Alexis, killing a couple of infected that were coming around the truck.

Jane looked beyond the truck and wanted to cry. *How are we going to get out of this?*

Past the truck was a huge horde of infected, heading their way. Emmett dragged Jane toward the truck as Alexis started it from the backseat and rolled down a window to blast the advancing horde. Jane could hear glass shattering behind them as the infected collided with the doors. They were only halfway to the truck and she didn't know how they were going to make it. The horde on the other side was almost at the truck, and there were also a few coming at them from the sides. Ana was helping Alexis keep them from getting too close to the truck and couldn't take out the ones coming towards her and Emmett.

Dropping the machete, Emmett pulled out his Beretta and made quick work of the five infected coming at them. Finally arriving at the truck, he opened the back door, giving Jane to Alexis, who was waiting to help her in. Holstering his Beretta and swinging the M4 off his back, he went around the front of the truck and began shooting at the infected closing in on them. Ana was doing a good job keeping most of them at bay with the compact MP5 from the back window. He made it to the driver's door, shooting three infected that were almost on him. Opening the door, he stopped, hearing a blood-curdling scream. He quickly looked through the truck to see that Jane was being pulled out of the backseat.

"Dad! Help!" Alexis yelled, trying to pull her mom back in.

It took a moment for it to register. *Under the truck!* When he crouched down, he saw the infected biting into Jane's leg. It ceased to move as Emmett shot it in the head. He jumped into the driver's seat and closed the door. Reaching into the back, he helped his daughter haul Jane into the truck.

"Shut the door! We need to get the hell out of here!" he yelled.

The door slammed and he switched it to four-wheel drive, putting the truck into gear. He stomped on the gas and they sped off, running over a few infected as they went. They still had to get out of the parking lot and he couldn't just barrel through the middle of the horde. There were too many of them. He skirted around the bulk of them but still ran over an increasing number.

"Hold on!" he said, speeding up.

A group of infected stood between them and the freedom of the open road. The truck slowed with the impact as dozens of bodies began to crash against the brush guard. Blood collected on the windshield as body parts flew up all around them, being torn apart by the aggressive tires. They crunched, bounced, and bumped over the last of them and turned onto the road leading to the interstate, passing the gas station that had been their original destination. He turned on the windshield spray and washed enough of the blood off to see through a small gap, although for the most part it just smeared worse.

They drove onto I-29 as the sun descended toward the horizon. After a few miles, Emmett pulled over. Getting out of the truck, he went to the back, opening the topper and tailgate

"She's unconscious," Alexis said, tears in her eyes as he opened the back door. "Dad...?"

"You have to stay strong for me, honey. I can't do this alone," he said as he took Jane into his arms and carried her to the tailgate. "Ana, take the rifle and get on the roof. Keep an eye out. Alexis, get the sheet from the bed back here and cut it into strips."

"On it," Ana said, as she grabbed the rifle from the backseat and climbed up.

Alexis took the sheet off the bed and pulled out her knife. Emmett cut open the leg of Jane's pants and looked at the wound, grimacing as he saw the missing chunk of flesh from her calf. Taking his belt off, he looped it around her thigh and tightened it down hard. He would get only one chance at this, and he quickly searched around in one of the duffle bags, pulling out a small hatchet. He looked at the hatchet and then hesitantly at Jane's leg, which was an odd feeling for him. The shock could kill her if this went badly, but she was worse than dead if he did nothing.

"We need to lay her on the ground," he said, setting the hatchet on the tailgate.

He picked her up and then laid her down on the ground. Alexis had the cloth strips in her hands. Her eyes roved from her mom to the hatchet and back.

"Dad, what're you doing?"

"We have to remove the bite from the blood stream. I just hope it's not too late."

Alexis's eyes grew wide, and she paled, "You mean…"

"It's the only option," he said confidently, having pushed past his hesitation. He had to act now or let Jane become one of them. "I'm going to need you to hold her down, just in case she wakes up."

"Okay," Alexis responded hesitantly.

"Ana, how are we?" Emmett asked.

"Good. The road's clear," she responded.

Emmett took the hatchet off the tailgate and approached his ex-wife.

7
CHOICES

"How long till we switch?" Connor asked, suppressing a yawn.

"Another hour or so. Can you make it, bro?" James responded.

"Yeah."

"You boys know I could take a shift," Felicia said from the backseat.

James looked back at her and smiled. "Nah, we got it. Manly pride and all that, you know."

She laughed, and James felt small butterflies flutter in his chest. *Oh, stop that*, he told himself, *you've only known her for a day*. There was no way he was already starting to like her. He wouldn't let himself. But when he thought about it, in high school he'd started liking girls just as quickly. That was his downfall, he figured. He was a hopeless romantic at heart and was always looking for someone.

James laid his head back in the seat and closed his eyes, trying to get some sleep before he was on the graveyard shift. He dozed off to thoughts of the pretty blonde woman sitting in the backseat.

"Wake up," a voice said, pulling James from his slumber.

He sat forward quickly, grabbing for any kind of weapon. They were surrounded! But then he awoke fully and saw that he was safe in his truck, not in a building full of zombies coming for Felicia and him. He shook his head, banishing the dream from his thoughts, and gathered his wits. All the lights on the truck were off and they were stopped on the highway. Connor was looking through the windshield with his 8x42 Vortex binoculars. James glanced toward where his brother was looking and noticed a group of lights in the distance.

"Where are we?" James asked, grabbing his binoculars off the dash.

"Just passed into Nebraska," his brother answered.

He noticed what looked to be a makeshift barricade in the middle of the highway ahead. There were lights all around the barricade, illuminating the armed people standing watch.

"Survivors?" James asked.

"That's my guess. But are they friendly?" Connor answered.

"That's a good question."

He was watching the men around the barricade, trying to get a feel for them, when his phone started to vibrate. He picked it up and looked at the screen.

"Hey," James said, answering the phone.

"Son, where are you?" Jack said, sounding tense.

"Just crossed into Nebraska. Maybe four or five hours away if we can go the speed limit."

"Good. At least you're getting close. Don't stop unless you have to. There are men here taking and killing people. Your mom and I are out of town, hidden in a barn. They're *hunting* survivors."

"Damn! We have something up ahead we need to take care of, but we'll get through and be on our way shortly. Hold tight, dad. We're coming."

"Sounds good, Son. I could take them, but we only have our handguns and an old hunting rifle."

"Don't worry about that. We brought the whole Andderson Family Arsenal, your AR included."

"Good, we'll stay low until then. Here, your mom wants to talk to you."

"Okay, love ya, Dad."

"Love you both."

There was a brief pause, and then he could hear his mom's voice. "You there, honey?"

"Yes, Mom. How're you holding up?" James asked, wanting to know his mom was okay.

His dad was a tough man and he would do what needed to be done, but his mom was more kind-hearted than all of the Andderson men combined.

"Oh, we're fine. Just doing a little camping in an old barn. How're you two holding up?" Diana asked.

James hesitated for a second and looked at his brother, who gave a subtle shake of his head.

"We're good. Getting used to this 'killing zombies' thing. It's actually kinda fun," he said, throwing in a little chuckle. She didn't need to know the full truth yet.

"You haven't just been killing zombies, have you?"

He never could hide anything from his mom. "We did what we had to do."

"I know, Son. There are a lot of things we've been having to do lately that we wouldn't normally. Just remember *who* is in control."

"Yes, Mom, I know. Where are you exactly?"

"You know your Great Uncle Tom's farm?"

"Connor, you know Uncle Tom's farm?" he asked his brother, who nodded to him. "Yeah, we know it."

"We're hiding in the old barn in the trees behind the house. You can't see it from the road. You have to come down the driveway."

"Good. Stay there and stay hidden. We'll be there soon. We have to go now, Mom. Love you and see you soon!"

"I love you too, Son. Let me talk to your brother real quick."

He handed the phone to Connor and went back to looking through the binoculars. They didn't look like crazy people. No body parts were hanging off them or anything like that. They just looked like simple people trying to survive in a harsh new world, but he couldn't tell for sure.

Something thumped on his window and he jumped, seeing a half-missing face peering through the glass. The zombie slapped its hand against the glass again, smearing blood on it as it tried to claw its way in.

"Come on, I just cleaned that," James mumbled to himself.

He rolled down the window enough to stick his hunting knife out and stab the zombie in the eye.

The zombie collapsed to the ground, and because of the angle he couldn't hold onto his knife, which was still embedded in its head. He cursed under his breath.

"Hey, bro, I need to get my knife. That zombie just took it."

Connor looked over, having just hung up the phone.

"What?" he asked, looking confused. "A zombie *took* your knife?"

"Yeah, its face did, and it didn't let go."

His brother chuckled, "Oh, okay. Let me get my gun and we'll make sure there're no more around."

Connor pulled out his handgun, which had a suppressor screwed onto the end, and James pulled out his new Remington 1911, also with a suppressor. They'd found it on one of the guys they'd killed in the shootout. It was their best find since the apocalypse started.

They looked around outside. Seeing nothing, they both grabbed flashlights and clicked them on, holding a flashlight in one hand and a handgun in the other. Getting out of the truck, they scanned their surroundings. After again seeing nothing, James crouched down and retrieved his knife from the zombie's skull, pulling it out with a sucking sound.

"Got it," James told his brother, displaying the knife.

"Good. It'll be hard to detour through the fields to get around that barricade."

"Yeah, I think you're right. I think I see a creek up there and a tree line."

"Guess that just leaves one option," Connor said, coming around and climbing into the passenger seat.

"Yeah, we have to go through it," James responded, going around to the driver's side. "Best prepare for the worst."

"Yep."

Connor picked up his brother's AR and handed it to him as James did the same. Connor reached into the backseat, pulling out his .308 rifle and setting it next to him while he held his AR.

"Think we should leave Felicia with the truck and go on foot? That way if things go south, we can always run into the night and get back here safely," James said.

"Could work, but maybe they'll be more likely to trust us if we show up in our vehicle with her," Connor said, pointing at the sleeping woman. "You know, instead of two heavily armed men showing up in the night."

"Good point. I'll be ready to tear through whatever we need to. You keep 'em in your sights."

They drove up, headlights illuminating the barricade in front of them. Felicia was awake in the backseat and they had filled her in on the situation. People moved around on top of the cars that formed the barricade. James could now see that the barricade was not just on the road but surrounded the entire settlement. It must have been a small town of survivors that had thrown up a makeshift fence to keep the zombies out.

They pulled to a stop in front of the semi, which was used as the front gate. Three armed men stood on top. They didn't have any serious firearms, only a couple of cheap hunting rifles and handguns.

"Stop there!" the man in the middle said.

All three of them had their guns pointed down at the truck. Connor was using his AR to sight in on the one talking just in case things hit the fan.

James showed his hands above the steering wheel. "We just need to get through. We don't want trouble."

"Then tell your guard dog to heel," the same man said, nodding in Connor's direction.

"Can't do that. We don't know your intentions or whether we can trust you. We just need to get through to our family."

"How can we trust *you*?"

James paused for a second. "You can't…"

The three men on top looked at each other and had a short, whispered conversation.

"If we let you in, you'll have to pay for the passage."

"What do you have in mind?" James said, setting his hands on his lap within reach of his handgun.

"You two look well-armed and capable. We're in need of some… exterminating."

The brothers looked at each other. "I think we can help with that, but why would we risk our necks?"

"As I see it, you have to get through. That leaves you two choices: you can kill us all or go around, which will take you quite awhile."

"What kind of 'exterminating'?" James asked, not sure if he liked the idea, but he didn't think they had much of a choice.

"We have a small hospital in town. It's overrun and we don't have the firepower to clear it. Won't take long, but we need to get in there."

James and Connor looked at each other and shrugged. They didn't have much of a choice. Either they helped these people to get through, or they killed them all, and James didn't like that idea. These people didn't seem bad, but he didn't trust them either.

He looked back at Felicia. "What do you think?"

"It sounds like it's our only option," she said, shrugging.

"Okay, we'll take your deal."

"Good," the man in the middle said, lowering his rifle and motioning his comrades to do the same. They hopped down off the semi onto some of the smaller cars and disappeared behind the barricade. The semi started up and pulled forward, leaving a gap that James could drive through.

Once through the barricade, he could see they did, indeed, have a small town that looked to be in pretty good shape. There was a main street running down the middle, with a total of twelve buildings—two stores and the rest houses. He could see people milling around, looking nervously at the newcomers. *Good,* James thought, *They'll be hesitant to attack if they're afraid of us... hopefully.* He pulled off the road into the parking lot in front of one of the stores and shut the truck off. Grabbing his AR, James got out to meet the man with whom he'd been talking. The man had left his rifle somewhere and was now only armed with a revolver in a holster on his hip.

"The name's Butch," he said, sticking his hand out.

James shook it. "James, and this is my brother, Connor."

Connor walked over and shook his hand.

"Where'd you guys get all that?" Butch asked, eyeing their gear.

"We've had it for years," James replied.

"You guys definitely know how to use it then. Where'd you come from?"

"Montana."

"How is it up there?" Butch asked, trying but failing to keep the hope out of his voice.

"It's just as bad, but it looks like you guys are doing pretty well."

"I'm glad it looks that way because we aren't. The vehicles only work so well against the roamers. We're in the process of building a more permanent wall, but we only have one side done. That's why we need your help. The contractor who was heading up the wall project was injured, and we need some of the medical supplies and equipment from the hospital. Not to mention it'll make everyone feel safer knowing the last building in town is clear."

"Honestly, we're glad to help. You have a good thing here and I hope it lasts."

"Thanks," Butch said, smiling a little, "I knew you two weren't all bad."

"Not always," Connor said with a smirk.

"Only when we have to be," James said, looking Butch in the eyes.

"Yeah… we've had to do the same. Always thought the end of the world would bring people together, not tear them apart."

"It gives evil men the excuse to be more evil," Connor said. "Shall we get on with it? We need to be on the move as soon as possible."

"Sure," Butch said, "It's on the other side of town. You can drive there and I'll meet you. Be ready for a fight. There're at least a dozen roamers in there, maybe even two."

"Oh, we'll be ready," Connor said, walking back to the truck, a smile growing on his face. He could get used to this kind of thing.

They got back in the truck and James slowly drove down the street, not wanting to make it seem like they'd try anything. The hospital was a relatively small building but still one of the biggest in town. They pulled to a stop outside, noticing they had guards posted around it—probably to make sure that if any zombies got out, they could take care of them quickly. Connor got out, opening the door for Felicia so he could get to their other guns.

"You guys sure about this?" Felicia asked when they had gotten all their gear together.

"What? You don't think we can take 'em?" James asked, smiling.

Connor knew what they must look like, all decked out in their gear. They wore full Kryptek camouflage like they always did, with their tactical vests full of ammo, their handguns, large knives, and tactical tomahawks. They both had their ARs in their hands and shotguns slung over their backs.

"No, I just don't want you getting hurt," she said.

"We'll be good," James said, "We know how to handle ourselves pretty well."

Connor could tell his brother had feelings for Felicia and he couldn't believe how easily James "crushed" on girls. Granted, it was the end of the world and eligible women would be in short supply, so he couldn't fault his brother for it. He just hoped it wouldn't be a weakness that got them killed.

James leaned in close to Felicia, whispering something in her ear, and Connor spoke up to cover the exchange.

"How many exits? You sure there're only two dozen zombies?" Connor asked as Butch walked up.

"There are two exits—this main one and the back door. We have them all locked up from the outside. There should be no more than two dozen. Between the staff and patients, we're only missing fourteen people, and I don't see how more roamers could've gotten in."

"Make sure we can get out those doors if need be. Just keep someone on them in case it's not us coming out. Could there be survivors?"

"I don't think so…"

"What do you mean 'you don't think so?' Yes or no? Could there be survivors?"

"Well…" Butch hesitated. "I guess there could be. We haven't been able to get in since it happened. But they would've had a hard time surviving in there. Plus, they never tried to get out."

Connor nodded. "So, highly unlikely. Good. That'll make things easier."

"But," James said, cutting in, "we would help them if we found anyone. Butch, I trust that everything will be in our truck and Felicia will be safe when we get back. Otherwise…" James let the statement hang in the air as he stared at Butch.

"You hold up your part and we will ours. That hospital is more important to us than a truck and a few guns."

"Good, then let's get those doors open. We have some exterminating to do," James said. He walked to the boarded double doors as two guys took crowbars and began to pry the wood off.

"We'll draw as many as we can to the doors, then head in. Tell your men to hold off and only shoot if they get past us," Connor said.

Butch nodded and relayed the order. Once the two men were done, Connor nodded to one of them and the man opened the doors. Prying the wood off had made quite a racket and he was hoping most of the zombies would be in the waiting room. He wasn't disappointed. As soon as the door opened groaning and scraping could be heard in the room and a stream of zombies began to pour from the door. The men from town began to scramble away, but the brothers didn't move. They didn't even flinch.

As soon as the first zombie stumbled out from the doorway, Connor sighted on its head and pulled the trigger. The AR jumped a little, but with the minimal recoil and the low power ACOG, he could see the back of the zombie's head explode as it fell to the ground, quickly replaced by another one. Before he could shoot again, that zombie was dropped by James. Now there were two zombies coming through at once, and he quickly found his target and pulled the trigger. A zombie dropped, and then another dropped, and he was on to his next target. When the brothers were done, there were ten zombies lying in the entryway, none having made it more than four steps out the door.

"Wow, I'm really glad we could work something out," Butch said from behind them where the rest of the men stood looking at them.

"Like I said, we've been shooting a long time," James said.

James nodded to his brother and they started toward the doors.

Connor was taking point, so he was the first one through, having checked all the corpses to make sure they were dead. He came into the room, flicking on the flashlight that was attached to the rails of his AR. He took a quick scan and walked farther in. His brother followed him in a second later. Their lights cut the darkness as they slowly moved through the large waiting room. It smelled like pure death with a hint of rotting flesh. There was blood covering everything—the floor, walls, couches—and everything was torn up. There had been survivors in here at one point. Someone had been fighting back.

They approached two corpses on the ground, which they shot in the head for safe measure. They still had their suppressors on and the sound in the room was muffled.

"That's twelve so far," James whispered from beside him.

James switched his partial magazine with a fresh one, Connor following suit. They needed to be ready for anything in here. Shooting zombies in the head out in the open was one thing, but in these tight confines *and* in the dark, that'd be a whole different animal. James motioned with his hand to the door on the left. They crept up to the door, Connor leading the way. James eased it open as Connor stepped through, quickly looking around. A noise to his right made him turn and sight on the zombie that was trapped under an overturned set of shelves. A casing fell to the floor as the bullet entered the zombie's head, ending its groans.

"Clear," Connor whispered, having checked the rest of the room.

James moved in behind him, sweeping the room also, just to be sure. It looked like it was used for storage. They moved to the next door on the opposite side of the room. They posted up outside the door and Connor nodded. James opened it as Connor went through. There were three zombies in the small examination room that immediately took notice and started towards him. He shot the nearest one, then the next one. Before he had a chance to aim at the last one, it was on him. He brought his gun up, keeping the zombie and its gnashing teeth at bay with the weapon held in front of him. It was trying to get at him past his gun when the back of its head exploded, spraying blood and brain matter into the air.

James came up next to him, "Sorry for the mess, bro. Thought you might need the help."

"Thanks. I'd rather be a little bloody than dead. But I don't think much got on me." Connor scanned the rest of the room. "Let's move on."

James nodded and they came up to the next door where they repeated their process, finding themselves in a hallway after exiting from the room.

They looked both ways. To their left was a dead end, with another door a little ways down across the hall. To their right, the hallway went down and turned a corner, heading back towards the front of the building. Connor motioned with his hand, pointing to the left, and they moved towards the door there. James brought up the rear, looking back at the rest of the hallway and making sure nothing came up behind them.

Connor moved into the open doorway and scanned the room. It was another exam room, only this one was clean. The room still looked neat and tidy. He made sure to shut the door, knowing Butch and his people would be glad to find a room that was still pristine.

So far, their mission hadn't been much of a challenge, and the brothers moved down the hall to finish clearing the hospital. They came to the corner and stopped dead in their tracks, hearing sounds. Connor poked his head around, keeping his light covered and trying to distinguish shapes in the darkness. He couldn't see anything, but he could hear *a lot* of shuffling and groaning coming from down the hall.

He came back around the corner and looked at his brother. Connor shrugged, and they both came around the corner at the same time. Their lights revealed over a dozen zombies trying to break through a set of double doors that led into the main room they had started in. As soon as their lights hit the zombies, they turned and started their slow march at them as the brothers began to pick them off one by one. They had four down before realizing they wouldn't be able to kill them all before the zombies were on them.

"The other end of the hall. We'll wait for them there," Connor said as he dropped another zombie to the ground.

James nodded and turned around, going halfway down the hall, then stopping to cover his brother. Connor followed, going past him and patting James on the shoulder as he ran to the door of the clean exam room. James came up next to him, and they waited for the zombies to come around the corner. A few seconds later, the horde began to swarm the hallway. The only problem was there were more now than what they'd first seen.

"There must have been more in the rooms down the hall!" James said as he began to fire.

"There has to be over two dozen of them!" Connor exclaimed as zombies began dropping to the floor.

They killed ten of them in the first few seconds, but still the zombies pressed forward, quickly gaining ground.

Felicia sat in the passenger seat of the truck, watching the men around her. The people seemed nice enough and had seen fit to leave her alone as they watched the hospital, but she felt uneasy about the whole situation. What if it was a trap? What if they knew the place was full of zombies and the brothers couldn't handle them all? Or what if there were more men waiting inside to kill them? Then what would happen to her? She shivered at the thought, remembering what James had told her before he left. He'd warned her to be careful and watch the townspeople, saying not to trust them and keep a gun close, just in case. "We'll be out soon," he'd told her, "Don't worry."

She *was* worried however. No matter what she told herself, she was worried for a lot of reasons. First, it was the end of the world and she wasn't sure how to come to terms with that. Second, she'd met these brothers who had saved her and made her realize that maybe the end of the world wasn't the end after all. Now here she was, alone and waiting for the only two people in her life she could trust, surrounded by a bunch of strangers who might try to kill her at any moment. She didn't know what to do or what to think, so she just sat there in the passenger seat, a rifle close at hand that she didn't even know how to shoot.

"I can't hold them much longer," James said, bracing himself against the door to the exam room.

Connor threw the exam table over on its side, pushing it towards his brother.

"Hop over this and prepare for some close combat," Connor said as he stood there, shotgun at the ready.

James let go of the door and jumped over the table, pulling his shotgun from his back to stand next to his brother. The door burst open and zombies began to pour into the small room.

Connor pulled the trigger and was rewarded as two zombies crumbled to the ground. James had his shotgun up and was squeezing the trigger as Connor pumped his shotgun. Two more zombies fell to the ground as he shot, followed by another from his brother and another from him. Connor had a pump-action and James had a semi-auto, but his brother could shoot just as fast as him. They stopped firing and the smoke cleared. In various positions on the ground in the doorway lay eight zombies, bleeding from holes in their heads.

"I think we finally got 'em all," Connor said.

He pulled some shells out of a pouch on his vest and began to reload his shotgun. James did the same as they walked over to the corpses, making sure all were good and dead. They moved out into the hall, swinging their shotguns onto their backs and grabbing their ARs, which hung from slings at their sides.

"So much for that room being clean," James said, looking back.

"Do you think they knew?" Connor asked.

"I don't know. There are a lot better ways to set a trap for someone. We'll see when we get out."

"Yeah, we will."

"Just remember, bro, we have to tread lightly. Whatever their motives, we need to get through."

"I know. I'm not going to do anything stupid. Just pisses me off. There were over four dozen zombies in here."

"Me too, but maybe they just didn't pay attention when it got overrun."

Connor grunted in response as they headed back through the hall and around the corner, still having two rooms to check. Both of these rooms were clear, all the zombies having already joined with the horde that had tried to devour them. Moving to the double doors, they removed a metal rod that barred them and exited into the waiting room, then went to the front doors but stopped when they heard shouting from outside.

"What the—?" James cut himself off as they heard a gunshot echo through the night.

"Let's go!" Connor said and barreled through the doors, gun leveled at the men outside.

Only, the men outside took no notice of them. They were all running towards the north side of town. Felicia sat in the truck, looking at them, relief plain on her face. Butch ran over to them and Connor kept him in his sights the whole way. They could hear more gunshots towards the front gates now.

"We're under attack. We need your help!" Butch said.

"Your hospital is clear," James said, AR still at his side.

"Yes, good, but we need you."

"No," Connor said.

"But—"

"I said no, or are you deaf? We risked our lives to clear your stupid hospital of the *four dozen* zombies inside. Now you want more? No. We agreed to your deal, and now we'll be on our way, one way or another."

Connor still had his AR in his hands, and while it wasn't pointed directly at Butch anymore, the meaning couldn't be missed.

"Fine, you want to leave? Then leave, but know that if we die, it'll be on your hands."

Butch poked James in the chest but he brushed the finger off.

"You have too little faith in yourselves. You've survived this long. Now, you may want to head to the front gates. They'll be needing your help," James said, going over to the driver's door and opening it.

Connor climbed into the backseat, never taking his eyes off of Butch.

"This is on you!" Butch yelled as he ran toward the front gate and the sporadic sounds of gunfire.

"Let's roll out," Connor said.

They pulled up to the semi that was used as a back gate. The big rig pulled forward and they sped out of town and into the night.

8
DEATH

"I know, I know," Connor said as James looked over at him from the driver's seat.

"What?" James asked.

"We should've stayed and helped them. That's what you're going to say, right?"

"Not at all. I was going to say 'good job.' We have to get to mom and dad soon or we'll be too late. Those guys can take care of themselves."

"Oh," Connor said, looking out the window.

"I do feel a little guilty," James said, "but we have to think about our own now. We have to focus on this group right here, our family."

"Am I part of that family yet?" Felicia asked.

"Of course!" James said, looking back at her. "Not like a sister or anything, more like a…"

"Like a…?" she asked.

"Well, you know…" He paused, searching for the words. "Oh, hey! A gas station," he said with obvious relief and pointed up ahead to a small, dark building with two pumps out front.

"Sure, change the subject," she said, rolling her eyes.

"What? We need gas."

They pulled to a stop next to the pumps and James looked around.

"We need to be careful here," Connor said. "Hard to see far in the dark with no lights."

"I'll keep the truck running. Let's make this quick," James said, getting out and looking around with his flashlight and handgun.

"Clear," Connor said from the other side of the truck.

"Clear," James repeated. He holstered his handgun at his hip and began to fuel up the truck.

"I could really use a restroom. I never had time at the last stop," Felicia said.

"Sure, let's make it quick," James said, coming over to Felicia's door and opening it. "Top it off and we'll be right back."

"Got it," Connor said, going over to finish fueling up.

"Now, stay close," James said.

They moved towards the gas station, Felicia with a machete and James with his handgun, the light from their flashlights cutting through the darkness and illuminating the path ahead. Creeping up to the door, James tried to look through, but the light reflected off the glass, making it impossible to see inside. He quietly opened the door. Catching movement out of the corner of his eye, he took a quick step back as a zombie came at him from just inside, which caused him to run into Felicia, who stumbled and fell down behind him. The zombie was through the door and its reaching arms were mere inches from his face when it was halted by a .45-caliber bullet that made a splendid hole in its head.

"Here," James said, turning and offering his hand to Felicia.

She took it and he hauled her to her feet, giving her a smile that she returned. Maybe there was something there after all.

"Behind you!" Connor yelled from the truck.

James spun around just in time to get hold of a zombie's neck as it descended on him, and the momentum of it pushed him to the ground. He lay on his back, struggling to hold the ravenous zombie at bay. In the light of his fallen flashlight, he noticed more zombies pouring out of the darkened doorway. He heard a gunshot, and one of the zombies dropped, but the rest kept coming. He brought his handgun up to the head of the zombie that was pinning him to the ground and blew its brains out.

As he pushed the motionless body off, he felt something on his foot and looked down to see a zombie biting on him, unable to penetrate the thick leather of his boot. He shot the zombie in the head, careful not to hit his own foot. Another zombie dropped next to him as he heard a shot from the truck. He could see at least half a dozen zombies around him and he aimed at the closest one, giving the undead a new hole to breathe out of. Immediately rising to a kneeling position, he took out another zombie and then glanced at the doorway, seeing movement inside.

"There're more in there! We need to go, now!" James yelled as he rose to his feet and took a step back towards the truck.

He glanced back, noticing Connor was at the front of the truck, shooting the zombies that were pouring out of the station, but he couldn't see Felicia. *Where is she?* Sweeping the area again, he noticed something just out of the light and rushed over to shoot the zombie that had hold of Felicia.

"Thanks," she said breathlessly as he helped her to her feet.

"Get to the truck!" James yelled as he turned and shot a zombie closing in on them. Then he shot another as his brother dropped one.

Felicia took off toward the truck and he aimed at a zombie between her and the truck, dropping it in its track.

"Behind you!" Connor shouted.

James spun around. He noticed vague shadows by the side of the building, so he quickly ran over, snatched up his fallen flashlight, and shined it in the direction of the shadows. This revealed a dozen zombies shambling towards them. He aimed and fired, dropping the nearest one, and watched as the next one fell from his brother's shot. Just as he acquired his next target, he stopped, his blood going cold.

A scream split the night and pierced right through his heart.

NO!

James turned around and watched as both Felicia and a zombie fell to the ground. He ran to her, shot the zombie, and dropped to his knees, pulling her head into his lap. Her eyes looked up at him pleadingly as blood poured from the side of her neck and she reached up to touch his cheek with a blood-stained hand.

"Please…" she whispered.

He brought his gun to her forehead and she closed her eyes, a look of pain on her face. As he pulled the trigger, her head jerked and her body relaxed in his grip. He stared at her beautiful face, once so full of life but now covered in blood with a bullet hole in her forehead. Something began to tear inside of him. It wasn't supposed to be like this! She'd only had a few more feet to make it to the truck.

A voice called to him from somewhere faraway, but he just knelt there, staring at her lifeless eyes. He hadn't loved her yet—he knew that—they'd barely known each other. But it was more than that. It was what she embodied to him—hope—a hope that somehow goodness could come from all this evil, that maybe there was still a chance at a life beyond just surviving. But all that was gone now, stolen away by a simple mistake.

My mistake.

"James, we need to go! Now!" a voice said. It was his brother's voice, and James snapped back to reality, hearing the urgency of his tone.

He looked up at the zombies and saw that they were closing in on him from all directions except one. Glancing down at her one last time, he laid her head on the cold, hard ground and rose to his feet, steeling himself.

This is not the end!

He ran to the truck and jumped into the passenger seat as his brother climbed in. Connor put the truck in gear and they raced out of the gas station.

"I'm sorry, brother," Connor said after an hour of driving in silence. James looked at him and wiped the tears from his face. "We still have each other. Don't forget that."

"It's my fault."

"How do you figure that?"

"If I'd just paid more attention, been more cautious of what was inside, maybe we *all* could have made it back to the truck."

"Look, James, I love you. But shut the hell up. You have no idea what you're even saying. You think you can plan for every outcome? Every decision? Grow up. You and I both know people are going to die. They always have, but now it's gonna be even worse. We have to be ready for that. *You* have to be ready for that."

They were silent for a long time.

"I need to know if you're good," Connor said.

"I am. It's just hard…"

"You can be sad. Hell, you can even cry more if you need to. I just need you to be ready to face whatever it is we have ahead of us. I can't do this alone."

"You won't have to. I'm here, bro. Trust me, I'm good."

"Well good, let's hear some tunes then. We should only be a couple hours from mom and dad."

James turned the music on and *Broken Pieces* by Apocalyptica began to play. *How fitting,* he thought as he prepared himself for what lay ahead.

James glanced at the phone as it vibrated and Connor picked it up.

"Hello," Connor answered.

A brief pause.

Connor's face fell.

"We'll be there in less than an hour! Stay safe. We love you both." He hung up and turned to his brother, "We need to get there now!"

"What's wrong?" James asked, already speeding up. The roads had been decently clear so far and he hoped it would stay that way.

"The men who are hunting survivors, they're at Uncle Tom's house. Mom didn't think they'd seen the barn, but they're at the house."

"Damn. We'll get there soon, and when we do, we'd better be ready," James said.

Connor nodded and climbed into the backseat where he began preparing their gear for a little "hunting."

They pulled onto the dirt road leading to Uncle Tom's house with their headlights off. Connor had his AR out the window, watching for any sign of movement as they slowly continued down the road. When they came around a line of trees, they saw two running vehicles parked at the house.

"Got 'em," Connor whispered, swinging his rifle towards the vehicles. James pulled the truck to a stop and grabbed his binoculars off the dash.

"I see four men and two trucks, and some lights in the field leaving the barn," he said.

"Plan?"

"Let's go back to the neighbor's house, then cut through the trees by the barn, get mom and dad, and get the hell out of here."

"Roger that." Connor nodded.

He backed the truck up along the road and into the neighbor's driveway, pulling to a stop next to the house and making sure to turn the dome lights off.

James quickly grabbed their mom's Ruger American .270 with a 3-9x40 Vortex scope and swung it over his back and then picked up his AR. Connor grabbed their dad's AR from the backseat. Jack's AR-15 was a basic Ruger with iron sights and a thirty-round magazine. Connor swung it onto his back and picked up his own AR.

"Let's do this," Connor said.

They took off through the field behind the neighbor's house, heading for the tree line that would lead to the barn. Hearing one of the trucks pull out of the driveway of Tom's house, they watched the taillights. The truck turned onto the road and headed to town. *Good. Fewer of them,* James thought.

Going through the field, they only encountered one zombie, which James killed with his tomahawk. Crouching in the trees, they looked toward the barn where their parents should be hiding. By the light of the moon they could make out two figures standing by the entrance a hundred yards away, armed with a rifle and shotgun.

"No!" James whispered, knowing these figures were not their parents. Connor flipped out the bipod on his AR and set it down on the ground while James did the same.

"Just like prairie dogs," Connor told his brother.

"Yes," James responded. He sighted on the left one while Connor sighted on the right.

"One, two, three…" Connor counted down.

The suppressed shots were separated by less than a second and the two bodies slumped to the ground. The brothers stood up and ran in a crouch to the barn. Arriving at the doors, they stabbed both men in the head with their knives. No need for them to come back and make life harder. James peered through the partially open barn door.

"You know, you could have made this a lot easier on yourself," a cold voice said from inside.

James froze. There were two men inside, one armed with a baseball bat and the other a handgun. Luckily, they had their backs to him, and he quickly scanned the room. It was a typical barn with a hayloft, stalls on the ground floor and everything covered in hay. There were six bodies lying on the floor, fresh blood pooled around them. He noticed a collapsed figure in front of the two men, but he didn't see anyone else in the barn.

He held up two fingers to his brother, who crouched next to him as they posted up outside the door. James rushed into the room in a crouch, stopping briefly to take aim at the man with the handgun. He fired and blood sprayed out the man's chest as he fell to the floor. The other man had just turned around when his brother's bullet took him in the abdomen, doubling him over.

The brothers swept the rest of the room—James the left side and his brother the right. James ran up to the slumped figure on the ground. It was their father, Jack Andderson.

"Dad!" James cried as he fell to his knees, looking at his father, who was bruised and bloody, looking like he'd been shot in the stomach and beaten nearly to death.

"Son," Jack said, his voice barely a whisper.

"What happened?" James asked, taking in his dad's wounds, tears brimming in his eyes. He wasn't a doctor and had no formal training, but even he knew his father was beyond saving. He reached down and grabbed his father's outstretched hand.

"They took your mother… she—"

He coughed and blood leaked out of his mouth. James didn't know what to do.

This cannot be happening!

"Your brother?" his dad asked.

His eyes were closed and James knew he was fading quickly.

"He's here."

Connor came over and took their dad's other hand.

"I'm here. Don't worry, Dad, we'll get her back," Connor said, a hard edge in his voice.

"I love you, boys… proud of the men you…" His voiced faded and he breathed his last.

James gripped his father's hand tighter. He could not, *would not* believe his dad was gone. With tears streaming down his face, he felt that same tear from Felicia's death rip even deeper into his heart. He could feel a part of himself dying and a hardness creeping in. How could God allow this to happen?

What was the purpose in this, the good that could come of it?

"We need to go now," Connor said.

Getting up and going over to the two men they had shot, Connor looked at them. He flipped the one over who'd been shot in the stomach and saw that he was still breathing. James stood up, wiping the tears from his eyes, and pulled out his knife. He looked down at Jack and knew he couldn't let his father come back as one of *them.*

When he was finished, he wiped the blood from his blade off and replaced it in its sheath as he walked over to stand next to Connor, who crouched by the wounded man.

"Tell me where they took her," Connor demanded. He shook the man, who just coughed and spit a glob of blood at him. "Suit yourself."

Connor shot the man in both legs and walked out the door. The man screamed weakly and began to roll around, grabbing at his legs. James kicked the baseball bat away and went over to the other man, picking up the handgun. It was a .38 revolver, his mom's handgun.

Damn them, he thought. He looked around the rest of the room, counting six bodies that had been there before they'd come in. At least their dad had put up a good fight; he'd been able to kill half a dozen of them before he'd gotten caught.

James walked out to stand next to his brother in the crisp night air.

"The men by the house," James said, "we'll get them to talk."

His brother nodded and they started towards the house.

The night was cool with dew on the tall grass as they crouched in the field behind Uncle Tom's house. They could only see one of the men in front of the remaining truck, smoking a cigarette in the light of the headlights. More than likely, four of the men had gone with the truck earlier, leaving only one unaccounted for.

"Maybe he's in the house," James whispered.

They crept around to the side of the house, staying in the tall grass. The man standing in the headlights wouldn't be able to see into the darkness. For all practical purposes, they were invisible as they stalked their prey. As they moved, they got a better view of the scene in front of the house. The truck was parked in the driveway. The man who was smoking leaned against the grill of the truck, looking out at the barn in the distance. On the other side of the house was an attached garage with the door open. Inside, the other man was scavenging around in a blue car.

"I think I heard something," the man with the cigarette said. "It sounded like a scream."

"Oh, shut it," said the other man. "Ain't nuthin' but the night playin' tricks on ya."

The smoking man grunted and took a long pull on his cigarette, blowing out a cloud of billowing smoke.

"I'll take the guy smoking. You kill the one in the garage," Connor said under his breath.

James estimated the man was about fifty yards away—a relatively easy shot. He sighted on the man's back as he rummaged around, took a deep breath and squeezed the trigger. The man slammed forward against the car and slid down the side, falling to the ground.

The man smoking looked over at his companion, "Fu—"

He was cut off as a bullet slammed into his shoulder, making him drop his cigarette and grasp the wound. Another round took him in the leg and he crumpled to the ground with a cry of pain. As the man squirmed on the ground, the brothers came out of the darkness into the light of the headlights. James looked around, making sure they had taken care of them all, while his brother kept his gun trained on the wounded man.

"I don't see any more," James said, coming over to train his gun on the man.

James threw Connor some rope he'd found in the back of the truck, and Connor caught it, leaning his AR against the side of the truck. He grabbed the man by the throat, yanked him up and slammed him against the grill. He pulled the man's handgun out of his holster and the knife from his boot and threw them away. He then took the rope and bound the man's hands behind his back. The man struggled a little at first but stopped when Connor punched him in his wounded shoulder.

"Now, we're gonna play a little game," Connor said in a voice that made even his brother shiver. He pulled out his tactical tomahawk and brandished it. "It's called 'how much do I hurt you before you tell me what I want?' Sound like fun?"

"Screw you," the man sneered.

"Alright."

Connor cut off a part of the man's shirt and shoved it into the man's mouth. He then slammed the spike of the tomahawk into the man's thigh and savagely ripped it out. The man screamed, but Connor slapped him in the side of the head with the flat of the blade.

"Let's try again. Do you want to play the game or not?" The man tried to say something but couldn't get past the gag in his mouth. "Just nod."

The man nodded.

"Good, now where did they take the woman from the barn?"

The man looked at him and said something that couldn't be heard through the gag.

Connor ripped the gag out, "What was that?"

"Why would I rat my men out?"

In response, Connor slammed the tomahawk into the man's side and jerked it forward, cutting a huge gash.

"I'm losing my patience!"

"Okay, please," the man said, gasping.

"Tell me, now," Connor growled.

"The courthouse. . . they took her to our base in the courthouse."

"The one in Linklon?"

"Yes, but you won't make it in time. They have a game they like to pl—"

The man's taunt was cut short as the blade of the tomahawk ripped through his throat. He grasped at the wound, trying in vain to stem the flow of blood. Connor casually walked over and collected the man's knife and handgun while the man slumped to the ground, the life draining from his eyes as blood pooled on the ground.

James looked at his brother with mixed feelings. He'd never seen Connor like this before, not that he could blame him. It had been the only way to find out and James would have done the same thing, but it was still a hard pill to swallow.

James looked at the man on the ground and noticed a red 'X' painted on his shirt with what looked like dried blood. He walked over to the man in the garage and rolled him over, noticing the same thing. At least they marked themselves so they'd be easy to identify and kill. James took the man's machete since they were one short and then he jogged over to the truck and noticed his brother looking around in the backseat.

"They don't have much in here. Just a bag with some supplies," Connor said, pulling out a yellow bag.

"Let's get to the truck then," James said.

They ran out to the road and back to James's truck, seeing nothing along the way. Connor threw the bag in the back seat and climbed in. James already had the truck started and they flew down the back roads, heading to Linklon, Nebraska.

9
SAFE—HAVEN

Sunday, post-outbreak day two

Emmett looked in the rearview mirror at the two women in the backseat and glanced over at the empty passenger seat. It hadn't been his fault, he knew that, but it didn't relieve the guilt he felt. Trying to save his wife had failed; in the end, shock and blood loss had killed her. He banished the thoughts. What happened had happened. There was no changing that now, only moving forward. He read the clock on the dash: ten forty-three. They should probably stop for the night. Pulling off the interstate at the next exit, he parked the truck on the overpass behind an overturned semi.

"Are we stopping?" Alexis asked, blinking the sleep from her eyes.

"For a few hours. If you girls want to get in the back and lay down, it'll be a lot more comfortable."

He shut the truck off and looked back.

"I'll be fine in here," Ana said, patting the backseat.

"Can I sit in the front with you?" Alexis asked.

"Sure, let me check the perimeter first."

He grabbed his Beretta and attached the flashlight onto the rail underneath the barrel. He flicked the light on and stepped out, scanning his surroundings. The underside of the semi made a wall to the north, while the guardrail helped obscure the view from the south. To the west was a parked car and the east was where they'd come from. Looking under his truck first, he then went over to the parked car. He shone the light inside and something stirred, raising a hand.

A survivor?

He pulled the door open and took a step back, a horrid smell invading his nostrils. The infected pulled itself from the car and thudded onto the road outside, definitely not a survivor. He shot it in the head, the suppressor muffling the sound. He checked inside, but there weren't any more. Walking around to the back side of the semi, he looked in the top of the cab. There was a body with its head bashed through the windshield. It wouldn't be coming back. He walked back to his truck and opened the door for his daughter.

Getting out, she gave him a hug.

"I miss her, Dad," she said, choking back a sob.

"I do too, sweetie. Your mom and I may not have gotten along the last few years, but I still loved her."

"I know, Dad. You did everything you could."

Emmett took a step back and looked his daughter in the eyes. He could see her grief, but she was far from defeated. He gazed into those hazel eyes and saw determination and a will to survive.

"I'm proud of you, Alexis. You've turned into a fine young woman and I couldn't be happier."

He pulled her back into the hug, feeling a surge of emotion. He usually kept those more in check, but with all that was going on, he figured the least he could do was let his daughter know how much he loved her. They stood there for an uncertain amount of time, silent tears streaming down Alexis's face. He held her and let himself feel all the things he had denied for years. A great sadness was washed away by the love he felt for his daughter. If he had to he'd destroy the whole world just to save her. Finally breaking the embrace, he stepped back and wiped the tears from his daughter's eyes.

"We should get some sleep. No telling what we'll face tomorrow," he said.

She nodded and gave him a quick kiss on the cheek. "I love you, Daddy."

She had a slight smile on her face when she climbed into the passenger seat. He walked around to the other side of the truck and shook his head. His daughter knew how much he disliked her calling him "daddy." He'd made a huge deal about how she was a grown woman now and should not address him like that anymore. But he had a sneaking suspicion she knew that he secretly liked it. He climbed into the seat and glared at her, and her smile widened as she closed her eyes and leaned the seat back. He was careful not to let her see his smile.

Ana was already sprawled out in the backseat fast asleep. It had been a long couple of days. He looked back at the young woman they had picked up. They'd been through a lot already, and he trusted her. She was skilled at shooting and killing the infected, and she'd be an asset for them, but he couldn't shake the feeling that she was hiding something. They hadn't learned much about her—just that she had some strangely sacrificial friends and walked around with an air of confidence. Ana was an anomaly and he was curious about her past. Not that it mattered much now. It was a whole new world and someone's past only mattered if it would help them survive. He leaned his seat back and held his Beretta in his lap. He would sleep for six hours and then they'd need to be moving again.

Emmett was moving before he was fully awake, his gun up and pointing out the window where the sound had come from. It was just an infected thumping against the back window, trying to get in. With the bars on the windows, it couldn't even touch the glass. He looked at the clock. He'd slept for six and a half hours.

I overslept, he thought, *I haven't done that in years*. He leaned his seat forward and turned the truck on. The girls stirred but didn't wake up. They could use a little more sleep. Putting the truck in reverse, he backed up. The infected tried to keep pace but couldn't. It was now in front of the truck, slowly coming at them with its arms outstretched.

He nodded to it. *Thanks for the wakeup call*, he thought as he ran it over.

They were back on I-29 a minute later, resuming their trek northwards.

Ana awoke, stretching and sitting up in the backseat.

"What do you have to eat?" she asked, yawning.

"Good morning to you, too," Emmett said.

"I'm starving," Alexis said, leaning forward and stretching.

He shook his head, smiling.

"We'll pull over at the next exit and have some lunch."

"Lunch?" his daughter said. "We just got up."

"Yes, but it's close to lunchtime. You two slept in."

Ana laughed. "Never thought that'd happen after the world ended. But I definitely needed it."

"I agree," Alexis said.

They pulled off at the next exit and Emmett did a perimeter sweep before he let the girls get out of the truck.

"All clear," he said. He walked back to the bed, climbed inside, opened the toolbox cabinet, and began to rummage around.

"Your dad wasn't in the military, was he?" Ana asked Alexis under her breath.

"Yeah."

"I never would have guessed."

Alexis laughed, "He's pretty strict sometimes, but you'll get used to it."

"What would you girls like? Canned soup? Some chips? MREs?" Emmett asked, showcasing each item.

"An MRE doesn't sound too bad," Alexis said. "What do we have?"

"Are they any good?" Ana asked her.

"It takes a little getting used to, but they're better than nothing, and filling."

"We have a few different meals. Why don't you girls come and pick them out?" Emmett asked.

"What are you going with, Dad?"

"Tortellini, as always."

"Then I'll go with that too," Alexis said.

"Me too," Ana said. "It actually sounds pretty good."

He came out of the bed with three green packages, gave one to each of the girls, and set his down on the tailgate. Opening it up, he pulled out all the contents—the main entrée, side dish, bread, dessert, flameless ration heater, and accessory pack.

"Wow, there's a full meal in that little package," Ana said.

"Everything you need to survive if you were out in the field. Perfect for the end of the world, too. Make sure to keep whatever you don't use or eat."

After twelve minutes of heating their meals with the ration heater, they were ready to eat. Emmett dug into his meal, not having eaten anything substantial in over a day.

"This is actually pretty good," Ana said, "Not bad at all."

"Growing up, Dad would cook once a week. Most of the time he tried to disguise MREs as real meals. Mom and I always knew, even though we never said anything. We got used to them over time."

"You girls knew?" Emmett asked. "I tried hard to spruce them up."

Alexis laughed, "Oh, we knew. Wasn't hard to look in the trash and find the MRE packages."

"Damn, I taught you too well," he said, chuckling, "Guess that's my own fault then."

They shared a smile, reminiscing on what life had been like before the divorce, and now this.

"What about your dad, Ana?" Alexis asked.

Ana picked at her food before answering. "He was a hard man, but he loved me. Wanted me to be tough for when he was gone. He always said, 'The world is a dangerous place, Ana. You have to be tough to survive.' When all this happened, he tried to get me to safety but was killed alongside most of his men. Those first few days were the hardest. We didn't know what was going on."

"What'd your father do?" Emmett asked.

"He was a… businessman."

He wanted to ask her more, but he knew she didn't want to talk about it. He figured it didn't matter much. If she didn't want to share, she didn't have to. They finished their meals in silence, putting the leftover items in a bag, which he put in one of the drawers. Then they got back into the truck and headed down the interstate once again.

The interstate was becoming increasingly difficult to navigate. So when they arrived at the scene of a massive wreck late in the afternoon, Emmett wasn't surprised. The vehicles were spread over both lanes, the median, and in the ditches. He pulled to a stop and looked it over. There was no way to go around or through it. Fortunately, there was an exit just ahead of them. Pulling out the map, he studied it. They could exit here and travel for a few miles down the highway to the town of Haven, Nebraska. Once through the town, they would have another couple hours and then they could get back on I-29. It would be a detour that would lose them a few hours, but he decided it was the best course of action.

"I want you girls to keep a gun close," he said, "and keep your eyes open. No telling what we might run into in Haven."

They pulled off the interstate and onto the highway. After a few minutes they passed a mileage sign with *Safe-Haven for Survivors* written on it with black spray paint.

"What do you think that means?" Ana said, eyeing the sign.

"Maybe the town is safe," Alexis said hopefully.

"Maybe…" Emmett said.

They arrived at Haven a few minutes later and he knew right away there was something different about the town. It was surrounded by a makeshift wall at least eight feet tall. He saw a watchtower at the front gate, and he noticed someone in the church steeple in the center of town. Cars with spiked poles sticking out of them surrounded the front gate. There were people on each side of the gate behind the wall and one in the watchtower, all armed with rifles. He pulled to a stop in front of the gate when one of the men held up a hand.

"Friend or foe?" said a new man, walking up onto the platform behind the gate. He had dark hair and was dressed in a white button-up shirt and black slacks. He had a friendly smile and carried no weapon.

"Friend," Emmett said, his hand on the Beretta at his side.

"Ah, good!" the man exclaimed, smiling widely. "Then we'll talk inside."

He signaled to someone down below and the gate was pulled open, allowing them to drive inside. There were two more armed men on the ground and one shut the gate behind them.

"You girls stay in the truck," Emmett said, stepping out. He looked around. The men on the wall went back to looking outside, but the two on the ground kept an eye on him. The man who had been talking walked up to him and held out his hand.

"Levi," he said, smiling genuinely.

"Emmett," he said, giving Levi's hand a firm shake.

"Nice to meet you, Emmett. You seem like a good group of people," Levi said, looking them over.

"Yes, sir," Emmett said.

"Is this your whole group?"

"Just us."

"That's too bad. We love guests here. But I'm getting ahead of myself. Welcome, friends, to Safe-Haven!" He spread out his arms with a flourish.

"Thanks. Haven't seen any communities still standing like this. It's impressive."

"We take a lot of pride in our accomplishment. Now, will you guys be staying or going on today?"

"Let me talk with the girls," Emmett said, walking back to the truck.

"Take your time. There's still plenty of light left. We don't open the gates after dark."

Emmett got into the truck and closed the door. "Do you girls want to stay here tonight?"

"What do you think, Dad?"

He thought about the question. He didn't trust them, but that didn't mean much. He didn't trust anyone. He didn't think Levi meant them any harm, though. They didn't seem like killers. But he knew from experience that some men didn't seem like killers until they were plunging the knife into their victim.

"We could just stay for a night, get a real meal, maybe even a real bed," Ana said.

"That does sound nice," Alexis said. "Dad?"

"One night then," he said, getting out of the truck and walking back to Levi.

"What've y'all decided?"

"We'll stay tonight, then be off in the morning. What are the accommodations?"

"Excellent! We have beds for all of you, adjoining rooms or same room if you like. Food is free the first night. After that we'll have to barter. You're more than welcome to stay as long as you like. We do have a few rules, of course. You'll have to follow those or move on."

"And those are?"

"Only handguns are allowed inside the walls. You can keep your other firearms in the truck, but you must park it in the parking lot. Keep your truck locked so others can't get into it. Other than that, be kind and polite to the people around you and we won't have any issues."

"Simple enough. Where's the parking lot?"

Levi pointed to the far end of town, "See the gate over there? You'll see a fenced-in area with some cars parked inside. I'll meet you over there and show you to your rooms." He stretched out his hand again. "We're glad to have you here."

Emmett shook it. "Thanks for the hospitality."

They drove through town, only seeing a handful of people. A settlement this size should have three to four times that amount of people living in it. But he figured with all that was going on, they were lucky this many had survived.

They pulled into the fenced area, which used to be someone's yard. The fence was chain-link and only six feet high, but they'd strung barbed wire along the top except for the gate. It wouldn't stop vehicles from plowing through if someone really wanted to, so he figured it was more for effect than practicality. The back gate to the town looked similar to the front, but there was only one guard on the wall and one on the ground. There was also no tower, probably because fewer people came from this way. He parked next to a Blue Ford Explorer. There were some clothes scattered in the backseat, along with some food items. Looked like whoever owned it was on the messier side. He turned the truck off and the girls got out, stretching.

"We have to leave the rifles here, but keep your handguns close and a melee weapon, just in case the infected get in. We always need to be ready to leave on short notice."

"I have all I need in my backpack," Alexis said.

He smiled. She always caught on quickly.

"I don't have anything anyway, so I'm ready," Ana said.

"You can borrow some of my clothes if you want to. I have more in the back of the truck. Or Mom's… you're about her size."

"Thanks, Alexis. I'd like that."

The girls went to the bed of the truck while he stood, taking it all in. His daughter had lost her mother but made a new friend, and she was taking all this rather well. She never ceased to surprise him.

He studied the town. If they had to leave on unfriendly terms, the back gate would be easier. It could possibly be rammed through with his brush guard. He figured he'd have no trouble getting out of the "parking lot" as there was no barbed wire on the gate. He was confident that if things went south he should be able to get them out. He hoped he wouldn't have to.

"Emmett!" Levi called, walking up to the gate of the parking lot.

"Yes?" Emmett said, walking over to him.

"One other thing. Get whatever you need out of your truck for the night. We lock the parking lot during the night."

"What if we need something?"

"You can grab whatever you need now. Otherwise, you'll have to wait till morning."

"Okay, I'll go tell the girls." Emmett walked back to the truck. "Grab whatever you need for the night. We won't be able to get into the truck."

"Why?" Alexis asked, getting out of the bed.

"We're in their town and they have their rules. I think they're afraid someone will come back here, get their guns, and start killing people. Either way, it'll make little difference to us. We'll have whatever we need with us."

Ana came out of the bed with a bag in her hands. "I have all I need now."

"Good. Alexis?" Emmett asked.

"Let me grab my bag from the backseat."

She went to the backseat while Emmett grabbed his go-bag out of the front seat. Inside he had a Glock 37, ammo, MREs, first aid kit, tarp, hatchet, change of clothes, and some other equipment. He kept this packed at all times, even before the apocalypse. He met the girls at the back of the truck, closed the tailgate, and locked the truck, sticking the keys in his pocket.

"Ready?"

"Yes, sir," Ana said.

"Yeah," Alexis said.

They walked over to Levi, who was standing by the gate, smiling warmly at them.

"Got everything you need?" he asked them.

"Yes," Emmett replied.

"Good. Now for the tour. I'll show you to your rooms. You can shower and relax for a few hours. Dinner will be at six in the Dining Hall across the street from your rooms."

"Showers?" Ana asked in awe. "Are you serious?"

"Of course. We have hot running water."

"Oh my…" Alexis said, "I was ready to never have a real shower again."

Levi laughed, "Well, you don't have to worry about that. We have our own water system here. We just ask you take a reasonable shower. No need to waste water."

"Sure, we can do that," Ana said, squeezing Alexis's arm. They were both grinning ear-to-ear. He didn't know if he'd seen his daughter this excited before, and it was just a shower. But it was all about the simple things in life now. The end of the world really had a way of changing one's perspective.

10
BREAKING

The brothers sped down the road to town, desperately aware of each second that passed. It would be getting light in an hour and they needed the darkness for cover. They had almost crashed twice now, but James had been able to dodge the zombies before they splattered against his brush guard and flew up through the windshield. His brother was in the passenger seat, ready with his AR, machete on his back. James's AR was next to him. Driving into town, they pulled into an alley two blocks from the courthouse.

"We gonna try to do this quietly?" James asked as he parked behind a dumpster. The white truck didn't blend in well, but it was currently dirty enough not to stand out too badly. He looked over at Connor, who sat with his eyes closed. "We got this, brother. We'll come out the other side. We have to."

"I know, just trying to calm down. I know if I go into this angry, it'll be hard to keep focused. We need to be at our best out there. Mom's life depends on it," Connor said.

He looked over at James, intensity in his eyes. James knew this could go very badly for all of them, but he didn't think about that. They couldn't—no—*wouldn't* fail. There was no other option. It was succeed or die.

"I will, brother. You won't see any hesitation from me ever again," James said, determined.

"I know. I'm not worried about that either. I have your back and I know you have mine."

"Yes, I do. We got this."

"Now, let's go kill those bastards and get our mother back!"

"Hell yeah!"

Connor got out of the truck and checked his gear. He grabbed his small daypack and threw it on. James also got out, grabbing the Mossberg shotgun and shoving it in a strap on the back of his tactical vest. They had taken the tactical, extended-tube Mossberg 500 shotgun from one of the guys outside the barn. He then grabbed his AR and shut the door, locking it and sticking the keys in his pocket. His brother looked at him.

"What? At least if it's locked and someone breaks in, the alarm will go off, and maybe make them hesitate."

They began to walk towards the end of the alley and James hesitated. His brother stopped and looked back at him.

"What?" Connor asked.

"I don't know, but do you think we should pray quick?"

James didn't *want* to pray. He was pissed at God right now. But when he thought about it, he still had his faith. He knew in his heart that God was with them, even in this. But he didn't want to think about that because it just brought up those painful questions. Why would He allow his father to die?

His mother to get taken captive? And Felicia? The world was in turmoil, but it was nothing compared to the storm that raged inside him.

"Sure," Connor said after thinking about it also. "Won't hurt, I guess."

"Lord," James began, "we ask that you continue to guide us and direct us. Protect us as we are about to enter the lion's den... Help us get Mom out safely. Protect her also. Lord... Be with the world, it's broken. If this is the end, then we'll be seeing you soon. Take care of Dad... Amen."

He opened his eyes and looked at his brother, who looked at him.

"I love you, bro," Connor said, embracing him.

He hugged his brother back, "I love you too, little brother."

"Little? I'm only two years younger, and you know I'm bigger than you, right?"

"Oh, I know. That's why you have the pack on, but you're still my *little* brother."

"Yeah, yeah, let's go already."

They jogged toward the end of the alley and the courthouse beyond.

"Locked and loaded," Connor said as he lay prone with his AR, looking across the street at the main entrance of the courthouse.

The building was a classic courthouse, with three stories, big steps leading up to it, and a domed roof. They'd been in the courthouse before when visiting family and remembered the layout. Inside was a big entrance room with steps leading to the top floor. The left side went around to the middle floor and the right had steps leading down to the basement. They would take down the men outside first, then go inside and head down. It was the creepiest place in the courthouse, and if the men they were about to face were psychopathic killers, that's where they'd take a prisoner.

"Let's rock and roll," James responded, lying next to his brother.

They'd counted a total of four men out front and had established an order for taking them out without the others knowing right away. It would be risky, but if everything went as planned, they'd have no problem. But things rarely went as planned.

James took the first shot, taking down the man standing on the left side of the building. Connor shot right after his brother, taking out the man by the front door. The man farther down the steps must have heard something because he turned around to see his comrade bleeding by the door. He was about to call out when a bullet took him in the neck, dropping him to the ground in a spray of blood.

Not quite where I was aiming, but that'll work, James thought. The last one was on the third floor balcony and would've been the first one they took out, but he was too busy sleeping in a chair to notice anything. He slumped a little when Connor's bullet took him in the skull. He'd never be waking up from *that* nap.

They lay there, watching the entrance and the sides of the building, waiting for anyone to come out. After a couple minutes they decided the plan had actually worked. James got up first and patted his brother on the shoulder, then took off across the street. He knew Connor was covering him while he ran, but he still stayed behind cover as much as possible. James made it to a car parked in the middle of the street and set his AR on the hood, aiming at the courthouse, covering his brother's approach. A zombie smacked its hand against the glass from inside the car but he didn't even flinch. He knew it couldn't get out and he was searching for any sign of danger. His brother pulled up next to him and patted him on the shoulder. James took his AR off the hood and his brother took his place as James ran towards the front door that was fifty yards away. He kept an eye out while going as fast as he could safely. He was almost there when the plan fell apart.

The door opened.

"Yeah, but I need a smoke and the boss—"

The man cut off as he noticed James running up the stairs towards him. The man brought his gun up, but before he could pull the trigger, a bullet ripped through his chest, exiting out his back and hitting the second man behind him. The front man crumpled to the ground, grabbing at his chest, while the second man went down on one knee. The .223 bullet hadn't had enough force left to do much damage to the second man, but it had stunned him. The round from James's AR was enough to put him down for good.

James slammed against the wall next to the door and peered inside to see if there was anyone else there but saw no one. He motioned to Connor, who took off running towards the entrance. A few seconds later his brother was next to him and they were moving through the door and into the courthouse. They saw nothing in the foyer.

"Let's reverse the plan—clear this floor first, go up, and then down," James said.

"Semper Gumby," Connor replied.

They moved to the left and began checking the ground floor, first entering the large center room, moving from left to right. After that, they cleared all the offices, encountering no one. They made it back to the foyer and climbed the stairs, crouching as they came to the top floor where they noticed makeshift beds lying around the large, open landing. Recognizing this floor as their sleeping quarters, they counted four men sleeping in the main room and a total of ten beds. There were four offices, all toward the back of the room. James motioned to his brother. Connor swung his AR to his side, pulled out his tomahawk, and approached the first man. He drove the spike into the man's skull, killing him quickly and quietly, then moved on to the next one, then the next one. He was at the last man when someone came stumbling out of one of the offices, rubbing the sleep from his eyes.

"Wha—" the man began.

James swung toward him and shot the man in the face, dropping him instantly to the ground. The last man began to stir, but it was too late. The tomahawk spike entered his skull and he knew no more. Connor quickly sheathed his tomahawk as they heard a rustling in the office to their right. A man came out armed and ready, or so he thought. He took two bullets to the chest—one from each of the brothers—and fell to the ground, never having fired a shot.

They waited before moving to the office on the left. James nodded to his brother and Connor opened the door. James barged into the room, gun up and ready. It was empty. They moved to the next room, stepping over the dead man. This room was clear, too. The next one was also empty, leaving the last one to the far right. Connor posted up outside and opened the door for his brother, who had taken a single step in when a blast ripped the door apart. James felt a sharp pain in his leading leg as he pulled back, leaning against the wall.

"I know you're out there. I'll blow you away if you step foot in this room!" a man's voice said from inside.

James pulled the shotgun off his back and stuck it around the corner without aiming, letting a blast off inside the room. He pumped and shot again, then again, and a fourth time.

On his fifth shot, Connor crouched down and poked his head around the corner, looking inside. He brought his AR up and aimed at the only hiding place in the room—the desk. He could see a foot sticking out from behind it, and while his brother was doing a great job with cover fire, he'd never gotten close to hitting the man. Connor put the chevron of his ACOG on the middle of the desk and pulled the trigger, hoping it wasn't too thick. It must have been because the man didn't even flinch, so he shot him in the foot. The man howled and Connor nodded to his brother, pointing at the desk.

James swept into the room, shotgun at the ready as he saw the man hiding behind the desk. He was circling to get a better view when the man saw him and began to bring his gun up. James blew his face off with buck shot.

James limped out of the room, his leg bothering him.

"Let's take a quick look at that," Connor said, coming over to him.

James leaned against the wall and slid down to a sitting position.

"Don't think it did much damage, but it sure hurts."

Connor lifted his pant leg and examined the wound.

"Looks like only two or three BBs hit. I think I can see them in there. They're not too deep. We'll have to look at it later, but for now you're not going to die or lose your leg."

"Good, because we're not done yet," James said.

Connor helped him to his feet and they went back down the stairs, keeping a sharp eye out. Whoever was left knew they were here now. Stopping at the top of the stairs leading down to the basement, they swapped out their partial magazines for full ones. They descended into the dark abyss.

No lights were on in the basement as they arrived at the bottom. The long hallway before them was completely shrouded in darkness. If they continued in the dark they might miss something, but if they used flashlights it would give them away. What they needed was some night-vision goggles or a thermal scope, but they had neither. They turned on the flashlights attached to the side rails on their ARs. Instantly, light burst into the darkness, banishing it. The hallway went down and curved to the left. There was a door on the left side of the hall that led into a big central room with an entrance opening to each end of the hall. When the hall curved to the left, there would be two doors on the back wall and one at the end of the hall.

Connor motioned towards the big central room on their left and James nodded. They would clear this one first. The door was already open, so they posted up on both sides of the door, with James crouching. They came around the door at the same time and wood splintered off the frame beside Connor. The sudden light from their high-powered tactical lights blinded the men inside, who had been waiting in the dark. James counted three men and took aim on the one closest to them, who had just fired the shotgun that went wide. James fired, taking the man in the left eye as his brother fired, killing the man in the back with a rifle. That left the last man in the middle, spraying wildly with the handgun. James sighted on him at the same time his brother did, and he was shot twice.

They'd stopped in the doorway for a few seconds, making sure they'd gotten them all, when James thought he heard something coming at them from down the hall. As he turned, he caught sight of a man raising a baseball bat a few feet away. He took a step back, swinging his AR around, and shot the man in the chest at pointblank. The man fell, dropping the baseball bat on James's foot, and he cursed under his breath.

He looked back at his brother and they went into the central room, sweeping left and right. They came to the door on the other side of the hall.

Across from them were two doors, with the third one being at the end of the hall to their left. No one was out in the hall. They went to the door on the far right, not wanting to have possible enemies behind and in front of them.

James posted up next to the door and Connor nodded to him. James opened it, and Connor went through the doorway, noticing the body of a young woman on the floor. She had been beaten and blood was pooled around her. He checked her pulse and she was barely alive. Looking her over once more, he assured himself that his assessment had been correct. She would never survive. They'd gutted her alive. He quickly brought his knife out and plunged it into the base of her skull.

"Find peace," Connor whispered as he gently laid her head on the ground.

He exited the room, shaking his head, and James glanced inside. They were both thinking the same thing now—this was looking less and less like a rescue mission. They came to the next door. James went to open the door but it was locked. He aimed his AR at it and shot the doorknob. It was empty of enemies but full of treasure. There were guns, food, ammo, clothes, and all sorts of valuables. A lot of it was useless now, except for all the guns and ammo. By the time they came to the last door, James was beginning to doubt that their mother was even here.

James opened the door and Connor burst through, gun at the ready. There was a man inside holding a handgun to a woman's head as he hid behind her body with only his head sticking out.

The woman was their mother, Connor realized, bloody and bruised almost beyond recognition.

"Now, now, let's—" the man began to say.

He stopped talking when the .223 round entered his brain and his body fell to the floor. Diana collapsed along with the man, not having the strength to stand. Connor rushed into the room with his brother close behind and went to his mother, cradling her head in his lap.

"Oh, Mom, what did they do to you?" Connor asked, tears forming in his eyes.

She was barely conscious as she reached her hand up, and Connor took it.

"I love you, boys," Diana whispered.

"We love you too, Mom," James said, coming over and kneeling down next to her, taking her other hand in his. Tears were falling freely down all their faces, making streaks in the blood and the dirt.

"Don't let this moment define you. Keep your faith. Promise me." She was beginning to have trouble breathing and they knew she had held on this long just so she could see her sons one last time.

"I promise, Mom. We will," James said.

He didn't feel the same tearing sensation he'd had when he lost first Felicia and then his father. No, he didn't feel that now. In fact, he didn't feel anything inside but a burning hatred.

Diana Andderson breathed her last and her two sons, the only surviving members of their family, knelt on the bloody ground and wept.

It was some time before either of the brothers had the strength to move.

"She might be turning soon," James said, pulling out his knife.

Connor looked him in the eyes and then shook his head, pulling out his own knife. James looked down at their mom and knew his brother was right. It was better for him to do it. Connor slid the knife into the base of their mother's skull. James no longer felt a burning hatred. No, the hate had turned into a calculated coldness. He would make them pay; he'd make them *all pay*!

James walked over to the fallen man and picked up the handgun, then joined his brother at the doorway.

"We should get all those supplies packed up to the entrance and loaded into the truck," James said.

Connor nodded. "Yeah, there are probably six full loads once we get things packed up. We'll be set for a while with all that."

James nodded.

The brothers went to the task at hand with numbness. They didn't think about anything—neither their current situation nor their next move. They just packed up everything they would need from the supply room and hauled it up to the entrance. When that was done, they went upstairs and grabbed all the weapons and ammo, going through the men's personal gear for anything useful. They all had those red Xs on their outer clothing, marking them as part of the gang, or cult, or whatever it was.

They had everything sitting down at the entrance when they went back to the truck, killing a handful of zombies on the way. The Red Xs must have cleaned out the town pretty well because there weren't many zombies roaming around.

James pulled the truck in front of the courthouse and shut it off. Connor began to haul the loot to the truck while James organized it in the bed and backseat. Their big backpacks were in the backseat, loaded with enough supplies to last them a week if they had to leave in a hurry. The rest of the stuff was organized by type in the bed of the truck in the totes, boxes, and bags they had.

Once that was done, they sat down on the front steps of the courthouse and stared out over the city as the sun began to brighten the early morning sky.

"Found these," James said, pulling out a box of Cuban cigars.

He handed one to his brother and then pulled out one for himself and grabbed the cigar cutter. They had the cigars lit when Connor pulled a bottle of rum out of his bag.

"Found this," Connor said, taking a swig from the bottle and handing it to his brother.

The sun rose behind them, casting long shadows in the street. Still, they sat there, the cigars running down and the bottle almost empty.

"What the hell do we do now?" Connor asked his brother as he flicked his cigar stub onto the sidewalk.

"That's a damn good question."

11
LOST SHEEP

Monday, post-outbreak day three

Emmett lounged on the bed in their room. He'd taken the first shower and been out quickly. The girls, however, were still in the bathroom after an hour. He lay on the bed, trying to decide if he felt safer here than outside the walls or not. On the one hand, they didn't have to worry about the infected, but on the other hand these people could turn against them at any moment.

The room Levi had given them was in someone's house, or had been before all this. They had the whole place to themselves, but they were just to use this room, leaving the rest of the house for other guests. It was furnished with two queen beds and included the connecting bathroom. There was a small nightstand between the two beds with a lamp on it and a dresser against the opposite wall. The only part he didn't like was the lack of windows, but it was the only room that could fit all three of them comfortably. He let his mind continue to wander and soon he was sleeping lightly.

Emmett bolted upright, hearing a door open, and noticed the girls coming out of the bathroom. The door leading to the rest of the house was still closed. He let out a sigh and holstered his Beretta. He hadn't expected to fall asleep.

"You girls ready?" he asked, getting off the bed and stretching.

"Almost," Alexis said. "I'd forgotten how nice a hot shower was."

"Ditto that," Ana said.

They spent the next few minutes grooming themselves. Emmett had the girls keep their handguns in their purses, which held some survival items also. He carried his Beretta openly as he didn't care if they saw it or not. He wore a clean black t-shirt and a pair of blue jeans with his combat boots. The girls had dressed in clean clothes, too. He smiled at his daughter. She had grown up so fast.

They exited the house and walked across the road which was illuminated by street lights. The Dining Hall, which used to be a café, sat in between two buildings that had previously been stores. He opened the door for the girls to go first, and then went in after.

The place was surprisingly busy. There were sixteen people sitting at the tables and booths. He noticed a table against the wall with a great view of the door and the whole café, which was close to the exit. They walked to it and he sat down where he could keep an eye on everyone. An elderly woman in an apron came over to them with three glasses of water.

"Welcome to the Dining Hall. Three meals?" she asked in a kind voice.

"Yes, please," Alexis answered, smiling at her.

"I'll be back in a few minutes with your food," she said, heading back to the kitchen.

"I wonder what it is," Ana said, looking around at the other tables.

He stopped listening as the girls continued to talk. He was scanning the room, trying to get a read on these people. Most of them seemed like normal people trying to adjust to life in a hostile world. Actually, it was surprising. Most of them seemed to be at ease and relatively calm. This community had gotten the walls up quickly, maybe even before the infection had begun to spread. Did someone here have inside information? He was pulled from his thoughts when the woman returned with three plates of food.

She set them down on the table. "Enjoy, and let me know if you need anything else."

"Thank you," Emmett said.

This place might actually be the real deal—a sanctuary full of good people safe from the infection. He looked down at his plate. It held mashed potatoes, corn, peas, onions, and ground beef, all mixed together.

"Shepherd's pie!" Alexis exclaimed. "I love shepherd's pie!"

They dug into their food and it tasted even better than it looked.

"Sorry, sir," Ana said after taking a couple of bites, "but this is a lot better than your MRE."

Alexis laughed and Emmett joined in.

"That it is," he said, sticking another bite into his mouth.

Once they were done they sat at the table with full bellies, feeling content and safe.

"I could get used to this," Ana said, leaning back in her chair.

"It *is* nice," Emmett said. "But this kind of living will make people forget what's beyond the safety of these walls.

"Yeah... but it's still nice," Alexis said.

Emmett casually watched the interactions between the people seated around them. Only a few of them had looked their way the whole time they'd been sitting here. They must see visitors quite often.

The door to the Dining Hall opened and a man dressed all in black with a white collar strode in. The priest came right over and sat down at the table next to Emmett and the girls.

"Well, good evening," he said. "I'm Father Ahaz. Welcome to our little community."

"I'm Emmett." He already didn't like this man.

"We're happy to have you here, however brief it may be. Did Levi inform you about our rules?" he asked, his eyes roving from Emmett to the girls, whom he eyed hungrily. No, he didn't like this priest at all.

"He did," Emmett said.

"All of them?"

Emmett hesitated.

"Ah, I see. Let me explain them now so we don't have any misunderstandings. There are ten, and I'm sure you've heard of them before." Father Ahaz went on to list the Ten Commandments, word for word as far as Emmett could tell. When he finished, he added, "The punishment for breaking any of the rules is death."

The way he said it made the hair on Emmett's arms stand up.

"We won't be here long enough to break your rules," Emmett said, staring the man down.

"I'm sure you won't, but if you do…" he paused as Levi came in the door and noticed Father Ahaz talking to them. Levi hurried over as the Father stood up. "I should be going. It was nice talking with you."

He walked right past Levi, ignoring him.

What the hell was that all about?

"I'm sorry if Father Ahaz bothered you," Levi said, coming over to sit down where the priest had been. "He likes to preach even when he's not in church."

"He's quite the character," Emmett said, watching the priest exit the Dining Hall. Right as he was about to leave, Father Ahaz turned back to them and shook his head. Something was seriously wrong with that man.

"He creeps me out," Alexis said, shivering.

"He's good at that, but trust me, he's harmless. He just likes to scare the visitors. Wants to keep his 'flock' safe."

Levi was smiling again, that warm, inviting smile. He seemed like a good man, a soft man. Emmett didn't think he would last long in this new world, but maybe if the walls held and… No, he wouldn't last long at all. It was a pity.

"Anyway," Levi said, "I just wanted to make sure you found everything to your liking."

"Oh yes," Alexis said. "The showers were amazing and the food was delicious."

"We really appreciate the hospitality," Emmett said.

"Good, I'm glad. If you need anything else, I'm just two houses down the street, number one-fifty-one."

"Thanks, we'll keep that in mind," Emmett said.

"You know, there's room here in Safe-Haven and we could use more people like you."

"Like us?" Ana asked.

"Yes, fighters, survivors," he said. He must have caught Emmett's raised eyebrows because he continued. "I'm not naïve. I know what we have here is rare and people will want to take this from us. We need people like you to help keep those people away. Otherwise, we don't stand a chance."

Emmett nodded. He couldn't agree more. "Sorry, Levi, but we have somewhere to be. I'll give you some advice though," he said, leaning in close. "Watch your back, and don't trust anyone. People will try to deceive you to get in here and then try to take it from the inside."

"You're saying I shouldn't trust anyone? Even you?"

"No, you shouldn't. We could be killers for all you know."

"Thanks for the advice, Emmett, but you're not evil. I can tell that much. But I'll keep that in mind."

"That's all I ask. You have something special here and it would be a shame to watch it go up in flames."

Emmett yawned and the girls joined him.

"The hot shower and food is putting me to sleep," Alexis said.

"I'll let you be for the night," Levi said, getting up. "Just remember my offer. We could give you a roof over your head, food in your belly, and all the warm showers you want. Think about it." He turned and walked to the door. "Oh, and breakfast will be at eight. Goodnight."

"Goodnight," Alexis said as she began to yawn again.

"I'm beat," Ana said, standing up. "I'm going to bed."

"I think we all should," Emmett said while also getting up. They thanked the woman who had served them before walking across the street to their room where the girls immediately plopped down on their bed, not even bothering to take their shoes off.

"You girls gonna sleep in your clothes?" Emmett asked, shaking his head to clear it.

His thoughts were foggy, and he was having trouble focusing. He must be a lot more exhausted than he thought. Alexis mumbled something in response but didn't move.

He went into the bathroom and splashed some cold water on his face, which didn't help. What was going on? *It's almost like... we've been drugged!*

He staggered over to his bed where his go-bag was sitting. He began to fumble inside, looking for his toiletries kit. *I might have something that...*

His thoughts trailed off as he fell to the floor, darkness closing in.

His head pounding, Emmett awoke lying on the cold floor. He blinked, willing his eyes to adjust to the darkness around him. He was in a small, bare room with a cement floor, no windows, and a single door. He rose to a sitting position and his head began to swim, so he leaned back against the wall and closed his eyes, waiting for the nausea to pass.

A few minutes later, he opened his eyes and looked around, noticing two figures lying on the floor. He looked more closely, trying not to move his head. It was the girls, and they were breathing. Taking stock of himself, he noticed his gun and boot knife had been taken, along with all the contents of his pockets. Where were they? What was going on?

Hearing a noise outside, he figured he would get an answer to those questions soon. The door to the small room opened and a figure stood tall against the light streaming in from the outside. It was the priest from the Dining Hall. Emmett wanted to lunge at the man and tear his head off, but knew if he moved he would be lying on the ground again.

"You come in here, into *my* flock, stained and dirty, and you think I'll just let you be? No, I cannot allow my flock to be tainted by your sinfulness. You will stay here until I can prepare for the sacrifice. You must pay for your sins," Father Ahaz said.

He turned around and closed the door behind him, plunging the room back into darkness. Mind racing, Emmett listened as he heard the priest's steps retreating up the stairs. They were in a basement somewhere, probably still in town. The priest wouldn't have risked leaving. Emmett had known he didn't like Father Ahaz, but he'd had no idea he was insane.

"Hello, is someone there?" a voice said from the other side of the wall.

"Yesss," Emmett slurred.

"I'm sorry..." the voice said.

"For what?" Emmett asked, his speech coming back to him.

"That you're here. This is the end," the voice said in resignation.

"What do you mean?"

"He must 'keep his flock clean by sacrificing the unworthy.' We're the sacrifice. And by that he means he's going to feed us to zombies. I'm the only one left for him to sacrifice tonight. He already 'sacrificed' the rest of my family."

Steps interrupted whatever the person was going to say next.

"It's time," Father Ahaz said.

"No, please! I'll repent. I'll change my ways. Just please don't—"

"It's too late for you, child. Your sins have tainted you." Emmett heard a zapping sound and something hitting the floor. "Get him up."

Shuffling and grunting sounded from the room, and he heard two sets of steps retreating up the stairs.

"Poor lost soul," Father Ahaz muttered under his breath as he followed.

He was feeding people to the infected to cleanse the sins of the town, and they were next.

12
DRIFTING

The Andderson brothers sat on the steps of the courthouse, lost and unsure of what to do. As the morning sun rose higher into the sky, a vehicle pulled onto the street half a mile down from the courthouse, bringing the brothers out of their stupor.

"Who do you figure that is?" James asked his brother. Connor looked through the ACOG on his AR.

"Red Xs," his brother said simply.

"Good. We'll kill 'em all," James said, trying to stand but sitting down again when pain flared in his leg. "Oh, right."

"I got you, bro."

Connor ran down to the truck and pulled out his .308 rifle, then ran back up the steps. Lying prone, he brought the rifle to his shoulder and scoped on the car that was beginning to slow two hundred yards out. James was lying next to his brother, AR at his shoulder.

"Ladies first," James said.

The car was slowly cruising towards them. James could see the four men pointing at the white truck when the shot went off. The .308 bullet punched a hole in the windshield and took the driver in the chest. The car sped up and swerved, crashing into a nearby light pole, and the three remaining men stumbled out of the wrecked car. James squeezed the trigger, but his shot went wide, hitting the car door next to the man he was aiming at.

Oops, guess I had a little more to drink than I thought. He reacquired the target, who had taken a knee to fire his handgun. *Doesn't he realize he wouldn't hit us at two hundred yards with that?*

The man next to his original target pulled out a rifle, and James aimed at him instead. He took his time aiming, ignoring the bullets that smashed into the concrete in front of them. He fired and the man went down, a bullet blowing through his lung. James swung onto the man with the handgun, but he was already on the ground, a pool of blood growing around him. Surveying the scene, he noticed the fourth man was down as well. Connor was deadly with that rifle of his.

James looked over at his brother, who looked back at him.

"Let's take a look at your leg," Connor said.

"Fine, now is as good a time as any. I won't feel it as much in my current state," James said.

"Yeah, I saw that first shot. What the hell?"

James shrugged, "You know I can't drink as much as you. I wasn't expecting more Xs needed to be killed."

His brother laughed as he returned from the truck carrying a first aid kit and some water.

"Take your pants off. It'll be easier to get at the wound. Otherwise, I'll have to cut them."

"Don't you dare cut my pants," James said as he undid his belt, then gently slid his pants down over the wound. "You better not let me die like this."

"If you do, I'll make sure to put your pants back on."

Connor poured a bottle of water over the wound, cleaning it. Then he looked it over, noticing there was some bruising but only two very small open wounds.

"Looks like just two BBs. I'll have to get them out."

"Oh, and I'm sure you'll hate doing it," James said.

"Causing you a little pain isn't gonna hurt me one bit."

"No, but it'll hurt me."

Groaning could be heard coming from the top of the steps as a zombie shambled their way. Connor looked at his brother and smiled.

"You better kill that freakin' thing! I don't have my pants on!" James said.

Connor chuckled darkly as he picked up his AR, shooting the zombie.

He set his AR back down and looked at his brother.

"Don't worry. I told you I wouldn't let you die with your pants down."

Crouching down, Connor pulled out the tweezers and spread the wound with his fingers, then stuck the tweezers in and grasped the small BB. James clenched his teeth and grunted. He may not be able to feel as much in his intoxicated state, but he could sure as hell feel his brother sticking the tweezers inside his leg. After a few minutes, Connor had both BBs pulled out and the wounds cleaned, irrigated, and wrapped in gauze.

"Doesn't look like it did much damage, other than the little holes and the bruising. My official diagnosis is you just need a good dose of 'toughen up buttercup.'"

They both smiled at that. It was one of their dad's favorite sayings. *Had been,* at least. He was gone now and so was their mom. All the mirth drained from them as they realized they had no plan, no purpose, and no reason to go all the way to Alaska if it was only them. It was supposed to have been their whole family.

James pulled his pants up and stood with the help of his brother. Putting weight on his leg, he realized it wasn't as bad as he'd thought. He'd be able to walk with only slight pain and a small limp.

They walked back to the truck.

"Might as well go get their guns, although we're collecting a small arsenal," James said, climbing into the driver's seat. He turned and started the truck; glad it was his left leg that had been shot and not his right.

"Should you be driving?" Connor asked, goading his brother.

"Shut the hell up and buckle up. No telling where we might end up."

Pulling over to the wrecked car, Connor got out and retrieved the guns and a bag of supplies. Once he threw the bag in the bed, he climbed back into the passenger seat.

"What now?" Connor asked.

They sat there in silence for a few minutes, the full weight of everything pressing down on them.

"I honestly don't know…" James said.

He knew they should pray for guidance and protection. But he just couldn't bring himself to. He was pissed at God for letting his parents die, for letting all this happen. He wanted to hurt those responsible for this—hurt them like he hurt—but he couldn't because they'd killed them already.

"We're pretty good at killing bad guys," Connor said, "and this is war, so let's go hunt the enemy."

"I like the sound of that. Let's head east and get on the interstate, then head north. Might as well work our way up still."

"It's as good a direction as any," Connor said.

"Hey, did you ever get ahold of Tank?"

"No. I tried his cell twice, nothing. I don't think he made it."

"Damn, he would have been a big help. East it is then," James said.

They drove back past the courthouse, noticing a few of the Red Xs had turned and were milling around outside. They pulled to a stop and killed them a second time, which made them smile. But their smiles were short-lived.

After driving down the highway a few miles, they saw three people scavenging around in a couple of cars. James pulled to a stop before the people realized they were there. It was two men and a woman, all armed and looking rough. Anyone would look rough right about now, and if they didn't, that might be more of a cause for alarm.

"Let's leave the truck here. No reason for it to get shot up," James said, turning it off and stepping out. His brother got out, too, and they walked towards the scavengers, who saw them after they had closed the distance to a hundred yards.

"What do you want?" one of the men yelled as all three turned around and aimed their weapons at them. The brothers already had their guns up and aimed, ready for any reason to drop these people.

"Just seeing what kind of people you are," James answered.

"What does that mean?" the other man asked, looking cocky. "We have more men around you, so I wouldn't try anything."

"Bluff," Connor whispered.

"Oh, I'm sure you do," James answered. "What are you doing here?"

"Why? Do you own the whole road?" the cocky man asked. The other man leaned in and whispered something in his ear, to which the cocky man nodded.

"I don't like this," Connor muttered under his breath.

"In fact, I don't think—"

A shot rang out, stopping the cocky man mid-sentence as he fell to the ground. James had the other man on the ground less than a second later. The woman just stood there, stunned.

"You don't—" James began but was cut off as she started firing and dove to the ground. He shook his head and motioned for his brother to go around and flank her.

Connor moved off in a crouch, sticking to the vehicles for cover, while James started to fire on her position, keeping her down. Connor made his way around to where he had a good view of her from seventy yards. He would give her one more chance, but she saw him and began to fire in his direction.

He shot her in the chest.

Her body crumpled to the ground and the brothers closed in on their position. One of the men was alive and groaning from having been shot in the gut.

"Help me..." the man whispered, looking pleadingly at them as they approached.

"Not my best shot, I admit," James said, walking up to the man and shooting him in the head.

"Get the guns and let's go."

They picked up two guns. One of the men had been armed with an airsoft gun spray-painted black.

Idiot. It'd gotten him killed in the end. They were halfway to the truck when they began to hear groaning. Looking around they noticed a horde of zombies heading their way from the east.

"Can't go that way!" James said as they hurried to the truck.

"There has to be at least a hundred of them!"

"Look at the map. See if we can get back on the interstate further north or south on one of the roads we passed."

Connor pulled out the map and flipped to the page showing Nebraska.

"Yes, we can go back a few miles, then turn onto Platte Road and head north for a hundred miles. I-29 comes to meet the road. All we have to do is pass through a small town called Haven. Should be an easy detour and we can be on the interstate within a few hours."

"Good. Let's go."

Night had passed and it was brighter in the room now, but not by much.

Must be a window in the basement somewhere outside this room, Emmett thought.

The watch on his wrist showed it was almost noon. When the girls had awakened, he informed them of what was going on and promised he would get them out. He still didn't have a plan besides rushing the priest when he came back, but he had to try something. No one had come after they had taken the man away to sacrifice him, but he'd heard the man's screams minutes later as he was eaten alive. His biggest worry was that they wouldn't come back until tonight and they would incapacitate him before he could try anything. Without knowing how skilled the priest was at keeping prisoners, it would be hard to tell how prepared he'd be.

"I can't believe this is how I go out," Ana said, breaking the silence that had lasted the morning.

"It isn't going to end this way, not while I'm still breathing," Emmett said.

"Do you even know what happened? How did we get here?" Alexis asked.

"My best guess is the food must have been drugged. I don't know who in the town is involved, but there are two others besides the priest for sure."

"Could be the whole town," Ana said.

"Could be, but Levi... If he's involved, he had me fooled," Emmett said.

"I liked him too, but I don't know," Ana said. "Some of the nicest people are cold-hearted. Father had this one guy, cold-blooded killer, but he was the nicest man I've ever met. I called him Uncle Zeke. Great guy, but he could kill with the best of them."

"What exactly did your father do?" Emmett asked.

She paused and then shrugged. "I guess it doesn't matter now, I just have a habit of keeping it secret. He was a businessman... only of the illegal kind. Ran a big family business."

"So, a mobster?" Alexis asked.

"Yeah, pretty much."

"Interesting. So that's where you learned to shoot. And those two men with you were your bodyguards?" Emmett asked.

"Yes and yes. They went everywhere with me, although they were more like big brothers. I miss them."

"I'm sorry," Alexis said. "What was your part in the mob?"

"Father had no sons, and, as such, he was mentoring me to take his place, which didn't sit well with the crew, but he had strict rules, and if he heard anyone talking bad about me, they ended up six feet under."

"I've known a lot of people in my life but never the head of a Russian mob," Emmett said.

Ana smiled, "Well, you do now."

"Let me guess," Alexis said, "your full name isn't Ana, is it?"

"Anastasia Romanovski, but that's too cliché, so I go by Ana."

"Definitely a mobster name," Alexis said, smiling.

"So what'd you do, Emmett?"

"I was in the Marines. After I retired I went into the private security business for a while."

"That makes sense. What about the truck? It looks like you were prepared for this, or do you just like overkill."

He chuckled, and then sighed, figuring it wouldn't hurt anyone now. He looked at his daughter.

"I didn't tell you the whole truth that night in the truck. I didn't want your mother to hear it all," Emmett said.

"That's okay. I could tell you hadn't told us everything. You may find it shocking, Dad, but I can read you pretty well," Alexis said, smiling.

"Is that so?"

"Yes it is, *Daddy*," she said with a wink.

Emmett burst out laughing. "You figured that out, did you?"

"Years ago, but I didn't want to ruin your gruff façade."

He laughed. *Damn, she's good.*

"Okay, I'm completely lost," Ana said, looking between the two.

"Long story," Emmett said. "But to answer your question, I worked private security for the company LifeWork for a year. In that time I saw... experimentation with a new drug they were developing. It was supposed to cure *everything*, which I, of course, thought was crap. When they tested the drug on rats, it would kill the rats. Problem was, they wouldn't stay dead. Then one day they tested it on a person... I confronted the owner of the company who denied everything, so I quit the next day and started prepping. I tried to get an investigation started but it never went anywhere. I knew no one would believe me anyway, but I made sure I was prepared, just in case."

"It's a good thing Mom never knew. It would have destroyed her."

Ana looked confused. "Why?"

"LifeWork was owned by Albert Hashen, my ex-wife's father."

"Oh, she didn't know?"

"No," Emmett said, leaning against the wall. "She never knew."

The afternoon passed with excruciating slowness. Emmett tried breaking through the door and walls, tried digging out, and even tried going through the ceiling, but the room was sturdily built and he could still feel the effects of the drugs in his system. He wasn't at his full strength. Even if he had been, he wouldn't have been able to break out.

All too soon, darkness began to engulf the room.

"Get ready. If anyone comes through that door, we'll rush them," he told the girls. "Better to die fighting than at the hands of the infected."

They nodded.

After a few hours they heard something above them and two people could be heard coming down the stairs. He looked at each of the girls and they moved to the front of the room with him in the lead. He would go through first and kill whatever was beyond that door with his bare hands.

13
SACRIFICE

Tuesday, post-outbreak day four

The town was small, with a main street running down the middle. The thing that impressed the brothers was the wall built around the whole thing. They even had working gates with a watchtower and everything. They'd counted twenty-six people down there, with eight guards on duty at all times— four at the front gate, one in the tower, one at the church, and two at the back gate, all armed with rifles, and they looked like they knew how to use them. The brothers lay on a tree-covered hill a few hundred yards to the south. It didn't give them a perfect view of the whole town, but they could see the main street and all the guard posts.

They'd pulled off the road after reading the sign: *Safe-Haven*. They hadn't believed it, so they climbed the hill with their ARs and Connor's rifle. They'd also each brought a set of night vision goggles. It had been their best find in the Red X's supply room. Well, besides the explosives still in the truck.

As the sunset painted the town orange and yellow, they continued to lay there.

"They look normal," James said, peering through his binoculars.

"They do... but let's give it a few more hours. Then we'll go down."

"Sounds good. Let's see what the night brings."

The door to the room opened and Emmett lunged at the man standing there. He made it halfway before he was hit with a Taser and fell to the ground, convulsing, electricity coursing through his body.

"No need for that. Your time will come," Father Ahaz said, standing behind the big man with the Taser. As Emmett convulsed on the floor, he realized he recognized the big man from the Dining Hall.

"Take the brunette," Father Ahaz said, pointing. "Alexis, wasn't it?"

The big man moved into the room and Emmett growled. He wanted to scream but his body wouldn't allow him. Ana lunged for the big man, but he swatted her aside. She hit the wall with enough force to knock her unconscious, and she crumpled to the floor. The big man continued to Alexis. She tried to fight back but his grip was tight and he put her in a choke hold until she started to blackout. He dragged her out of the room and the priest tied her hands behind her back then put a chain around her neck with a leash attached to it. She blinked the blackness from the edges of her vision, taking hurried deep breaths.

"There, now you look the part. Did you know your sins are like chains, dragging you down to hell? No? You will shortly." He pushed her forward with a command, "Walk."

She looked back at her father, lying on the ground, unable to move, and tears began to form in her eyes.

"I love you, Dad," she said, trying to keep the primal fear out of her voice.

Emmett's mind raced. How could he get to her if he couldn't move? There had to be *something* he could do.

"Oh, and Emmett," Father Ahaz said, glancing back at him. "Listen for the screams. It'll mean your daughter is paying the price for her sins."

The big man shut the door and the last thing he saw was his daughter being led to slaughter at the hands of a madman. He tried to move, tried to scream, but his muscles wouldn't respond. He laid there, tears streaming down his face. How could this happen? To come so far only to have his daughter ripped away from him now. It wasn't right.

As control of his muscles returned to him, he sat up and began to pound on the door.

Damn that man!

As he sat in the cell, he heard a voice filter down from above and he renewed his pounding. Either the door would break or his fist would. He couldn't make out the words but he knew that voice. It was Father Ahaz.

It was drawing close to midnight before the brothers noticed anything unusual. As if by some unspoken signal, people began to stream out of their houses, gathering in front of the local church. The church stood in the center of town, east of the road, and on the front lawn was a strange, fenced-in area. It looked to be a new addition as the lawn was tore up inside the fence. People gathered around the front of the church like they were waiting for something.

"This is odd," Connor said as he looked through the ten-power scope of his .308 rifle.

"Yeah, it is. Maybe this little town isn't so sleepy after all. Keep your eyes—wait—are those zombies?"

They were bringing zombies out on leashes and putting them into the fenced-in area on the lawn. They set loose six zombies inside the fence, and then closed the gate. The zombies pressed against the fence, trying to get at the people on the other side, but the fence held.

"What the hell?" Connor said.

"I have no idea…"

James's sentence trailed off as the door to the church opened and a man all in black with a white collar stepped out. The priest was not alone; he was leading a woman with brunette hair by a chain. Her hands were behind her back and it looked like her face was wet. Was she crying?

A voice rose from the town and the brothers could barely make it out.

"My flock, it's time to appease God by sacrificing this sinful woman to cleanse our sins." It was the priest talking.

"Oh, sh—"

"He's going to do it," Connor said, cutting James off. Connor swung his crosshairs onto the priest.

James knelt there for a second, looking in horror at the scene before them, then made a decision.

"Screw it! Cover me. I'm going in. Get that priest down."

"Roger that. I'll take him once you get in. Watch your back, brother."

They shared a look and then James burst into action. He grabbed the NVGs from the ground, leaving the daypack and his binoculars. He put the NVGs on his head and pulled them down, heading toward where he had seen a conveniently placed tree that he thought he could use to climb over the wall. He made it to the wall limping only slightly and climbed the tree, hearing the priest continue to preach. He couldn't make out the words, but there was something about hell, condemnation, and being cleansed by the blood of sinners. *Crazy son of a...*

He got over the wall and slipped behind a house on the other side of the street from the church. He could see through a gap between the houses to the street beyond. The guards had even gathered in the circle. In fact, the whole town was there. He crouched down and slowly made his way between the houses toward the main street, flipping his NVGs onto the top of his head. With the lights illuminating the street so well, he wouldn't need them.

"We must appease God and sacrifice her to the demons he has sent to test our faith!"

The priest sounded like he was getting to the end of his speech. James aimed at the man and got a front-row seat as the priest's head exploded. The sound of the gunshot arrived a moment later and everyone just stood there in shock as the priest fell forward and rolled down the steps of the church. The captive girl acted first. She shoved aside the big man standing by her and darted inside. Then all hell broke loose.

The big man moved next, turning and heading after the woman. He fell as James's bullet took him in the back. The rest of the gathering broke into chaos, with people screaming and running for cover. He swung onto the next armed man, who was turning in the direction of his brother outside the wall. He went down as a .223 bullet ripped through his chest and James noticed another armed man go down in the crowd. The armed men returned fire, shooting wildly into the night in the direction of Connor—they didn't realize there was a wolf in their midst yet.

Whether all these people were bad, or only the priest, was irrelevant. If they were willing to sit by and let innocent people die, then they deserved what they got. *Like this guy. He gets a bullet to the neck and he deserves it. Four to go*, he thought as he noticed another man fall to the ground, clenching his chest.

"Get to your houses and stay inside!" a man shouted to the crowd.

James briefly looked at him, but he was unarmed, so he went looking for his next target. He spotted an armed man crouched behind a street light and shot him in the head. He heard another gunshot but didn't see the man fall. He knew his brother hadn't missed, however, because he'd heard the sound of the bullet hitting the body. It made a very distinct *whack* sound.

By this time, most of the crowd had dissipated except for the two armed men who were left, and they had taken cover on the side of the church. Those remaining men had realized there were two shooters and were hiding from both of them. James turned and went behind the building to his left and down a few houses to get a different angle on the men. He came up in a different gap between the houses and saw one man hiding on the side of the church. He crouched, aiming at his chest, and let his bullet fly. The man fell against the church wall, leaving a red stain against the white-painted wood. The last man broke from cover and tried to make it inside the church. He made it to the top of the steps before a .308 bullet tore a hole through him.

James noticed two men emerging from a house, a shotgun and revolver in their hands. He aimed at them, noticing the one looked like the father and the other the son. He shot the man with the shotgun—the father—in the stomach. He fell to the ground and his son grabbed him and began pulling him back towards the house. *Good, that should keep the rest of them inside.* He went back over to where he had climbed over the wall just as his brother dropped down next to him, tossing him the daypack. He shrugged the pack on and went to his brother.

"I'll make a break for the church. She went in there," James said.

"I'll cover you," Connor said, AR in his hands and his .308 slung on his back.

James took off across the street and burst into the church. It was empty, so he turned around and motioned for his brother to follow him over. His brother ran through next to him and James shut the doors, locking them. That would at least slow them down if they came after them.

"Let's find her and get the hell out of here, and quick," Connor said looking around at the church.

It was a large-roomed church with two rows of pews and a podium up front. There was only one room off to the side in the back—probably the dead priest's office. He nodded to Connor and they began in that direction, scanning for any enemies inside. They made it to the door and posted up outside like they always did. James opened the door and his brother went in.

"There are stairs leading down," Connor said as he came around the corner. "I hear voices. Best prepare for more."

Emmett checked on Ana. She was alive but unconscious, with a bloody spot on the back of her head. Laying her in a more natural position, he went at the door with crazed determination. Trying to break it down with his shoulder had proven useless. Kicking it had yielded the same result, so he sat there pounding on it with his bloody fists once again. He could hear the priest talking, but he tried to shut the noise out, not wanting to hear his daughter being eaten alive. When the gunshot ended the priest's speech, hope soared in him.

Seconds later it sounded like a war was going on outside and then he heard footsteps coming down the stairs. He crouched by the door, ready to fight to his last. Instead, he was greeted by a voice he hadn't expected to hear ever again.

"Dad, it's me," Alexis said outside the door.

"Alexis honey, are you okay?"

"Yes," she said, a quiver in her voice.

"Can you get us out?"

"I'm trying, but I need to get my hands untied first."

"What is going on out there?"

"I don't know, but someone shot the priest and I ran inside."

He leaned against the wall. His daughter was alive, but for how long? The chances that the people shooting were here to help were very slim. They probably wanted the town for themselves, and they were going to take it, one way or another.

There was a lull in the gunfire.

"We'd better prepare for the worst. Are you free, honey?"

"Almost," she said. He could hear her rustling around outside the door.

He heard a thump above, a pause, and then a gunshot from farther away. So there were at least two of them, but it was probably a group of four or more to take on the whole town. He waited for a while but heard nothing else.

"Hurry, sweetie."

"There, got it!"

She opened the door and he crushed her in a hug that drove the air from her lungs. For a moment, in her father's arms, it was like it used to be before the world fell apart.

"I thought I lost you," he said, a tear slipping down his cheek.

"I love you, Dad."

He took a step back and looked at her face. She looked scared but relieved. He slipped the chain off her neck and let it fall to the floor.

"I love you, too."

The doors to the church closed and they could hear footsteps upstairs. He quickly looked around for any kind of weapon but there was nothing. The priest had cleaned the place out. He'd noticed that they were in some sort of basement with two other rooms next to theirs. Maybe he could find something…

There's no time.

"Get behind me," he told Alexis.

Two figures descended the stairs, rifles at the ready. He was taken aback for a second, thinking the military had come for them. They wore camouflage with tactical vests fully loaded, NVGs on their heads, and suppressed AR-15s in their hands. He was impressed. Whoever these two were looked like they were ready for war. They came to the bottom of the stairs and stopped, keeping their guns pointed at them.

The shorter one wearing a backpack stepped forward, lowering his gun. "We're here to rescue the girl. Who are you?"

"The girl?" Emmett asked.

"The brunette behind you, the one the psycho priest was going to feed to the zombies," the other man said. He was slightly taller and built more solid than the other and had some sort of high-powered rifle on his back that looked like a Remington.

"That would be my daughter," Emmett said.

"So you're a captive, too?" the shorter man asked, looking to his companion.

"Yes."

The taller man lowered his rifle but eyed him warily. They didn't trust him, and he respected them all the more for it.

"Give us a quick rundown of what's going on here," the shorter man said.

"We were passing through and decided to stay here for the night. They drugged us and threw us in here. The priest is sacrificing people to the infected."

The shorter man opened his mouth to answer and then shut it, listening. "There are voices up there. We need to get out of here. Can you shoot?"

"Yes, we both can," Emmett said.

"Bro, I don't—" the taller man began.

"We have no choice. We have to trust them," the shorter man said. He walked over and handed Alexis the pistol from his hip. "Here."

The other one reluctantly came over and slung the rifle off his back. "Are you a good shot?"

"I'm a Marine," Emmett said.

"Semper Fi," the taller man said, handing him his rifle. "You should know how to use this then."

Emmett looked at them more closely. *They're brothers*, he realized.

"Let's go," the shorter brother said.

"Wait," Emmett said. "We have one more, but she's unconscious."

"Can you carry her?"

"Yes. Alexis honey, take the rifle." They traded guns and he stuck the pistol in the back of his belt. He went back inside and picked up Ana. "Ready."

"Stay behind us, and keep your heads down," the shorter brother said.

The brothers started up the stairs and Alexis followed with the rifle. She checked the chamber as she went up, her dad carrying Ana behind her.

James led the way, with his brother trailing behind. He could definitely hear voices outside now.

"This might get nasty," he told Connor.

"We'll kill them all if we have to."

"Yes, we will."

They moved to the front of the church and looked out one of the windows. The man who'd been giving orders earlier was in the street, still unarmed. There were four armed men around him, having picked up the weapons lying on the ground. The brothers moved to either side of the doors and motioned for the other three to get down behind the nearest row of pews.

"We can work this out. There doesn't have to be any more bloodshed," a voice said from outside.

"That's Levi," the girl, Alexis, whispered to them from behind the pew.

"What makes you think we want to work this out?" James said through the doors.

"I didn't want to hurt Emmett's group," Levi said. "I tried to talk to Father Ahaz, but he wouldn't listen. I had no choice."

"What do you mean you had no choice? You stood by as the psychotic priest fed people to zombies," James said.

"But what was I supposed to do? He was the one truly in control here. I was just the public face for strangers."

"You could have acted. How much blood is on your hands because you did nothing, Levi?"

"Too much…" Levi said, subdued. James was looking at him through the corner of the window and he truly looked defeated.

"Lay down your weapons and walk away, and we'll leave here without killing all of you."

"How can I trust you?"

"You can't, but how many unarmed people did we kill? It's that or you all die."

Levi stood there, looking at the four men around him. Then he looked to the church and straight at James.

"Give me your word and we'll lay down our weapons and leave."

"Levi," one of the men said, "We can't just—"

"Enough!" Levi said, ripping the gun out of the man's hands. "Your word?"

James looked to his brother, who shrugged.

"You have our word. Lay down the guns and go back to your houses, and we'll leave and never return."

"And we want our gear back," Emmett said, speaking up.

Levi threw the gun down in front of him and the three other men reluctantly did the same.

"Eli, go get their things."

The man who had spoken before moved off, huffing as he went. James and Connor nodded and opened the doors, keeping their guns pointed at the three unarmed men.

Connor gave a little wave of his hand, shooing them. "Go. Be gone before I change my mind."

The three men glared at him but walked off. Levi, however, stood there.

"I'm sorry, Emmett," Levi said as Emmett came out carrying Ana.

"Save your apologies and be glad I don't kill you where you stand. You tricked us, lured us into the trap." Levi tried to speak, but Emmett interrupted him. "Save it. If you say anything else, I'll shoot you right where you stand."

Levi stood there but said nothing. He just shook his head and looked behind him. Eli returned, carrying their bags. He set them down at the bottom of the stairs and went to stand next to Levi.

"Levi, you stay here till we're safely out. Eli, you can hit the road," James said, walking down the steps. Eli looked to Levi, who nodded, and he took off towards one of the houses.

"I have a truck over in the fenced area," Emmett said, pointing. "Watch the girls, and I'll go get it." He looked to Levi. "Where are the keys?"

Levi motioned to a fallen man and Emmett went over and grabbed the keychain off his belt. He glanced at his daughter, hesitant to leave her alone again, but he trusted the brothers, so he took off at a jog over to the parking lot.

Connor stood there, wanting to shoot the man standing before them. He was such a coward—letting a madman run the town while he lured people in to kill them. Who would do that? But he didn't kill him. In this new world, he knew the man, Levi, wouldn't last long. His brother was also aiming at Levi, so Connor swung his AR onto his back and walked over to the fence where six zombies were groaning and trying to get at them.

"Bro?" James asked.

"Just taking care of these," Connor said, motioning towards the zombies with his tomahawk.

"Got it," James said, his attention back on Levi.

Connor walked up to the first one and smacked it in the side of the head with the blade. It crumpled to the ground and he moved on to the next one. After a few seconds, six corpses lay inside the fence.

"You may want to do the same to your men, Levi," Connor said, coming back over to stand by the unconscious auburn-haired woman.

"Why? They haven't been bitten."

"Doesn't matter. Seems like some of them turn, regardless. But suit yourself. We'll be out of here long before it's our problem."

A truck started up inside the fence and pulled out, heading their way.

James couldn't help but admire the truck when Emmett pulled up. It was a black Ford and looked like it had been made just for the apocalypse. He kept his gun on Levi while Alexis grabbed their bags, throwing them in the backseat. She held the door open as Connor carried the unconscious woman over, laid her down in the backseat, and closed the door.

"We're parked to the south. We'll get the gate, then jump on and ride out with you," James told Emmett.

"Okay," Emmett said as Alexis shut the door and Connor started for the gate across town.

"Let's go, bro!" Connor yelled.

"Well, bye," James said to Levi.

As they ran through town, followed by Emmett in his truck, they made sure to keep an eye out for anyone who might try something, but they arrived safely at the gate and Connor opened it while James covered him. He wasn't truly worried about the townspeople. If they were spineless enough to let a madman sacrifice people to zombies, they wouldn't try anything now.

The truck pulled through the gate and they jumped on the running boards, holding on through the open windows as Emmett took off down the road. James looked back to see Levi walking down the main street towards the open gate.

They made it to their truck within a minute. The brothers hopped off as Emmett pulled to a stop and stepped out with his daughter.

"I don't think I can thank you two enough for saving my daughter," Emmett said as he walked around the truck, handing them their guns back.

"No need. We're just glad to help and get a few more bad guys killed in the process," James said. "I'm James, by the way."

"Emmett," he said, shaking James's outstretched hand. He had a firm grip.

"Connor," his brother said, also shaking Emmett's hand.

"And this is my daughter, Alexis."

She shook each of their hands in turn.

"The one in the truck is Ana," Alexis said.

"Where are you off to now?" James asked when the introductions were over.

"We were going north, but we'll have to adjust since I'm not going through that town again and the interstate is blocked to the south."

"Well, that throws a wrench into our plans, as well. We were heading that way. It's probably going to be easiest to head west on I-80 to I-25, and go up through Wyoming. That should get us there. We'll just have to do some detours to avoid the big cities."

"Since we're all going in the same direction, we could caravan," Alexis suggested.

"It's not a bad idea," Emmett said.

James looked at his brother, who gave a subtle shake of his head.

"Sorry, but no. It's just my brother and I now," James said as Connor began to walk back to the truck.

"Really? Why wouldn't you want our help?" Alexis asked.

"More people mean more food, more noise, and more weakness. We're a two-man team, not a group," James said.

"But—"

"Honey, let them go," Emmett said. "Thanks again for the help."

"No problem," James said. "Who knows? Maybe we'll see each other sometime in the future. Not like there are many good people out there anymore."

"Farewell," Emmett said, stepping back as the brothers pulled out in their truck.

"Adios," James said, waving as they drove by. He rolled up his window as they headed south towards I-80.

"Don't you think—" James began.

"Nope," Connor said. "They would just slow us down, especially with two women."

"Yeah," James said.

His mind flashed back to Felicia and he felt a pain in his chest. He couldn't be hurt if he didn't let anyone in, and he was determined not to let anyone in again. They had their mission—search out survivors and help them, whether that was food, water, or a bullet to the brain.

Connor turned their Apocalypse Road Trip playlist on and *Road to Nowhere* by Bullet for My Valentine started to play. James couldn't help but think about how much had changed since they'd started this trip. They'd been so naïve. Now, as they sped down the road, he swore to himself he would never be like that again. They would save everyone who needed saving and kill anyone who got in their way. It was them against the world.

"We ride together," James said.

"We die together," Connor responded.

"Badass brothers for life," they said in unison.

EPILOGUE

The Andderson brothers were driving down I-80, the sun rising behind them, when James's phone rang.

"What the...?" he said, picking it up and looking at the number. "Hello?"

"So you bastards are still alive," a familiar voice said on the other end.

"Tank? Is that you?"

"Of course it is! Who the hell else would it be?"

"Holy crap, man! We didn't think you were still alive! Where're you at?"

"That's a damn good question. I'm heading north on I-25 with a few friends I made. I remembered your plan and we decided it was as good as any."

"When did you leave?"

"Just now. Took us a long time to get out of the city. It's a bloody mess back there."

"I bet. We've been sticking to more rural places. Anywhere not infected?"

"Not really. Most of North America is gone. There are a few places left, but they're rare."

"Damn, dude, it's good to hear your voice. I'm glad you're alive."

"Yeah, me too. It got close there a few times, but 'ol Frostmourne got me out of those situations."

James laughed. "So what's your weapon situation? Vehicles?"

"The weapons are pretty slim—a few firearms with little ammo. We have six vehicles with us now and about twenty people."

"Wow, you got out with a decent-sized group then."

"Yeah, we had a lot more to start with, but those damn undead took half of 'em."

"Damn, but we're glad you got out."

"I'm just glad to be leaving that damn city in the dust. How you guys lookin'?"

"We are sitting pretty well. We've collected a lot of weapons with plenty to spare. We're driving my white RAM. Oh, and there's a souped-up black F-450 rolling somewhere behind us. They're friend-lies. It's just Connor and I in my truck. We lost Mom and Dad."

"That blows. I feel for you guys."

"Thanks, we'll need to stay in touch. If we lose cell service, then you can leave messages on the road signs."

"Sounds like a plan. You guys stay alive now, okay?"

"We will. Same to you. And Tank, be careful. The people are worse than the zombies."

"I'll keep an eye out. We may stop somewhere safe and wait for you. How long till you catch up?"

"Maybe a day, depending on how much ground we can cover."

"Well, I'll be in touch. Talk to you guys soon."

"See ya, Tank," James said and hung up the phone. "You're not going to believe who that was."

"Bro, I've been sitting right here the whole time," Connor said.

"Oh yeah. Well, it was Tank. He's alive and traveling with a few friends on I-25. They're out of FoCo and heading north. We should be able to catch up with them."

"Hell yeah. It'll be good to have him along."

James focused back on the road. *Tank is alive. Well, that's something at least.*

They rode in silence for a while, each absorbed in their thoughts. They'd lost their parents and it had been a heavy blow. But that was not all there was to live for. There was more. There *had* to be more. Every time James closed his eyes, he saw Felicia resting in his lap with a bullet hole in her forehead, their father lying dead, and their mother tortured and dying. He wouldn't be able to easily forget them or the pain that came with losing them anytime soon. But maybe, just maybe, he could move on, if a little.

They pulled off the interstate and into the closest truck stop. Stopping at the pumps, James jumped out and stuck the nozzle in the truck.

"Damn prepay," he muttered. He hung the nozzle back up and walked around the truck to where Connor stood. "We need to go inside."

"We need water anyway. Let's do this carefully."

They walked up to the front doors and began to beat on them. After giving it a good minute or so, Connor stepped back and James opened the door. A few zombies piled out and they made quick work of them. Afterward, they went inside, flicking their flashlights on to see in the semi-darkness. They made their way over to the counter where James turned his pump on and then they went to the back room where, luckily, there were over a dozen cases of water and some sports drinks.

"Jackpot! Grab one of those carts and let's load it up."

A few minutes later they were wheeling the cart to the front door and James opened the door while Connor pushed it out. When he exited behind his brother, he saw that Connor had his AR aimed toward the truck. James quickly did the same, noticing a black truck parked on the pump opposite theirs. An auburn-haired head popped out from behind the truck.

"You guys mind turning pump three on?"

It was Ana, the redheaded woman with Emmett's group. Connor grumbled something and went back inside while James pushed the cart to the back of their truck, then went over to the pump, sticking the nozzle back in the gas tank and beginning to fill it up. He then moved to the back of the truck and unloaded the cart.

"Alexis told me what you guys did for us," Ana said, walking over. "Thank you. She also told me about how badass you two were, which I, of course, didn't believe. But it does look like you might know a little about what you're doing."

"You're welcome. We've been planning for this for years. Just never thought it'd actually happen."

"Yeah, pretty crazy, isn't it?"

"Indeed. So, what're you guys doing here?" he asked as Alexis got out of the truck and came over to stand by them.

"We decided we would just follow you. You could use our help, whether you know it or not," Alexis said, standing with her arms crossed.

"Is that so?" James said, raising an eyebrow.

"Yes, it is."

He chuckled. "Well, we can't stop you from following us."

"What happened to you guys anyway?" Ana asked as Connor returned, carrying a few grocery bags of food.

James was silent as his brother walked up and threw the food into the bed of the truck.

"We recently lost our parents," he said, "and not to zombies."

"I'm sorry. I lost my mom a few days ago," Alexis said.

"Seems like we've all lost loved ones," Ana said.

"There's more water in there. You want some?" Connor asked, eyeing the girls.

"I'll come grab some with you," Ana said, following Connor back inside.

"Where's your dad?" James asked Alexis.

"He stayed in the truck. Didn't want to get in your way. He respects your decision to go it alone."

"So you convinced him otherwise?"

"Well, Ana and I. We figured there had to be a reason, and I'm sorry about your parents, but we can help each other. Will you just try it for a few days?" she asked, giving him what he figured were the notorious "puppy dog eyes."

"I'll have to talk to my brother, but a few days couldn't hurt," he said. This woman was full of fire and determination.

"Good. At least you'll think about it."

Ana, followed by Connor, emerged from the station carrying bags of food with a cart full of water. He brought the bags over to Emmett's truck and loaded them into the bed while Ana wheeled the cart over, then came back to their truck, Ana trailing behind.

"So what'd he say?" Ana asked as Connor settled next to his brother.

"That I'd have to talk to my brother," James said.

"Good. That's what your brother said, too. So, do you two want to lead the caravan for now?" Ana asked as she walked back to the truck.

"We never said if we agreed or not," James said, exasperated.

"Well, either way we'll be following you till you stop next," Alexis said.

Connor shook his head and climbed into the bed of the truck, rummaging around in the totes from which he pulled out two sets of radios and chargers. Getting out, he handed one of each to Alexis.

"This way we can at least coordinate. If you're going to follow us, then you're going to follow our lead. Got it?" Connor said.

"Sure. I'll let my dad know."

"Good," Connor said, going to the passenger seat of the truck and leaving James and Alexis at the back.

"We'd better get going. 'Burnin daylight,' as they say," James said.

Alexis chuckled. "My dad says that all the time. And I think you'll be surprised at how well we operate," she said, walking back to the truck and climbing into the passenger seat.

James walked to the fuel pump and topped off the tank, then jumped into the driver's seat and gave a nod to Emmett, who nodded back.

"Is this thing working?" Ana said over the radio Connor held.

"Roger that. Rolling out," Connor responded.

"You were in the military, too, weren't you?"

"Yes, miss, I was."

"Never would have guessed."

James chuckled and Connor looked over at him, trying to hide a smile. The trucks pulled out, the white Ram leading the black F-450. *Turn the Page* by Bob Seger was playing on their playlist. Maybe there was still hope after all.

ACKNOWLEDGEMENTS

I couldn't have finished this book without the help of all of the people listed below, a huge thanks to:

Jesus, who is my ultimate inspiration in everything.

My wife, for all your help with editing, the cover, and making me write even when I didn't want to.

My family, you've always been there for me and supported me in this.

Guildies in the FRG, for all your hard work helping me polish things off!

My awesome editor, you helped make this book readable.

My cover artist, you brought the image in my head to life.

And finally all my readers, you are the ones who keep me going and allow me to chase this dream!

ABOUT THE AUTHOR

Joshua is a Jesus Freak and follower of the Way. As an adventurous nerd, he loves the outdoors and when he's not found high in the mountains of Alaska, he can be observed living on the rolling plains of eastern Montana with his wife, guns and two katanas. He has a passion for all things imaginary and finds inspiration in the wilderness, away from all the distractions of life. Some of his other passions include hunting, shooting, board and video games, hard rock, movies, reading and the Walking Dead.

Learn more about Joshua at:
www.joshuacchadd.com

Also by Joshua C. Chadd

The Brother's Creed Series
Outbreak
Battleborn
Wolf Pack
Bad Company (Coming Soon)
Book 5 (TBA)